TITLE _Tales to Keep You Up at Night_

AUTHOR _Dan Poblocki_

06/06/60	01/13/74
03/09/62	11/21/83
˙65	12

Tales to Keep
You Up at Night

DO NOT READ
THIS BOOK

TALES TO
KEEP YOU UP
AT NIGHT

BY DAN POBLOCKI
ILLUSTRATED BY MARIE BERGERON

Penguin Workshop

PENGUIN WORKSHOP
An imprint of Penguin Random House LLC, New York

First published in the United States of America by Penguin Workshop, an imprint
of Penguin Random House LLC, New York, 2022

Text and the illustrations on pages 182 and 191 copyright © 2022 by Dan Poblocki
All other illustrations copyright © 2022 by Penguin Random House LLC

Visit us online at penguinrandomhouse.com.

Library of Congress Cataloging-in-Publication Data is available.

Printed in the United States of America

ISBN 9780593387474

1st Printing

LSCC

Design by Mary Claire Cruz

For Lilith,
with loving gratitude—DP

TABLE OF CONTENTS

AMELIA IN THE ATTIC

Amelia discovered the old book lying in a dark corner of her grandmother's otherwise empty attic. Its paper jacket was missing—the cloth cover a faded red, almost pink. Embossed in silver on its side was a long title that appeared blurry in the dim light. Amelia was struck, however, by the bright white sticker at the bottom of the spine. Someone had typed numbers on it and adhered clear tape to keep it from falling off. She recognized the numbers. Dewey decimals. When Amelia flipped open the cover, she found a paper pocket glued inside, a blue card sticking crookedly out of it. Each line on the card had been marked with purple stamps—days, months, years—going back decades.

What was a random old library book doing up here?

Her grandmother had not resided in this house for a long time, and Amelia missed her with all her heart. If the last due date stamped on the card was correct, Grandmother would owe the library a hefty sum, unless library fines disappeared when *you* disappeared.

Amelia held the book up to the bulb at the top of the steep steps. The title on the spine glinted again in the light—clearer now. Amelia looked closer.

Tales to Keep You Up at Night.

The title was familiar somehow.

A shiver passed through her.

Grandmother had been interested in science and history and memoirs of writers and artists. Scary stories? Not so much. Amelia wondered if Grandmother had left this book up here on purpose.

When she turned to the steps, there was a skinny silhouette staring up from below. Amelia flinched, then blushed. It was Winter—her little brother. She hadn't recognized him at first because yesterday, Mom had shaved his head after he'd wiggled during a haircut and her scissors slipped.

Amelia had come up to the attic in the first place partly because Win had been pestering her. Recently, he had lost both of his front teeth and had somehow taught himself a shrieking type of whistle that he alone thought was *hilarious.*

"What are you doing?" he asked.

"None of your business," she answered, brushing past him, keeping the book hidden at her hip.

"Want to play a game?"

"I want to be alone."

"But I'm *boo-oored*," Win whined.

"You could help Mom and Mama with Grandmother's things."

"Never mind!" he yelled, and took off running down the hallway.

In the ancient house, his every footfall felt like an earthquake. She shut her eyes and let out a long breath. Winter had only been a piece of the reason she'd sought out the attic. The night before, Amelia had dreamed she met with Grandmother up there. She couldn't remember much of what happened in the dream. Only bits and slices. But she did remember the dream feeling intense enough that it made her wish to come up and explore.

Was *that* why the book felt familiar? Had she seen it in the dream?

Downstairs in the foyer, cardboard boxes lined the walls. Amelia's mom was placing paper-wrapped parcels into one of them, and her mama was in the kitchen, pulling dishes off the shelves and lining them up on the countertop.

"What have you got there?" Mom asked.

"An old library book." An idea struck Amelia. A way to escape her brother for the afternoon. Keeping her voice low so Win couldn't hear, she added, "I'm going to go return it."

"Good idea, sweetheart," Mom answered distractedly. Amelia's family had been at Grandmother's old house all weekend, preparing for its sale. Her mothers were both running on fumes. "The library is just down the street."

"I know where."

"Take Win . . ."

Amelia opened the front door and slipped outside, pretending to not hear. A brisk breeze mussed her long hair. She zipped up her green canvas jacket, clasping the faded hardcover to her chest.

"Look both ways!" Mama called out from down the hall.

"I will!" Amelia promised.

The door swung shut as Win peeked from the top of the stairs.

Down the sidewalk.

Around the corner.

Amelia skipped over the cracks in the concrete, concerned slightly about that old rhyme and her mothers' backs. You know the one. Then she paused and considered what might happen if she decided to not be so careful.

Amelia was hiding a secret anger, something she hadn't even shared ith her best friends, Scotty and Georgia. She hated that Mom and Mama were clearing out Grandmother's house, that they were going to sell it. What if Grandmother came back a year after she'd disappeared to find the place empty, her memories discarded? Wouldn't that only make the time she'd been away from everyone who loved her even harder? Amelia wouldn't share her frustration with her mothers. Whenever they came to a decision, they stuck with it, no matter what anyone else said, especially she and Winter.

The question of Grandmother's whereabouts had haunted the family since she'd gone missing. One year earlier, Grandmother was supposed to have arrived for lunch at Amelia's family's home, a few towns over, but she'd never shown up. When her mothers went looking for Grandmother, they found her car in the driveway and her house in perfect condition. But there was no sign of her and no clues to where she had gone. The police visited over and over, asking a bunch of questions that the mothers kept from the kids. Amelia begged to know what they'd thought was going on.

Mama and Mom had told Amelia and Winter that Grandmother might have been secretly struggling with a health issue. Dementia, they called it. They'd explained that as certain people grew older, sometimes they became confused. Their brains got sick. Betrayed them. Their memories failed. Sometimes they couldn't recognize loved ones. If they weren't under proper care, sometimes they wandered off.

Mama and Mom were certain dementia was the answer. But Amelia wasn't so sure. Shouldn't there have been some kind of a clue that Grandmother had been ill? Grandmother had known who Amelia was during a visit the week before the disappearance, and her memory had been perfect. She could recall events from her childhood as if they'd occurred only yesterday. As far as Amelia knew, Grandmother hadn't once gotten lost walking, shopping, hiking, or driving to pick up her grandkids for an overnight.

The scary thing, they said, was that in Grandmother's town, there was a creek whose banks rose high during storms. Sometimes, the muddy water rushed ferociously, carrying away fallen branches and bug-eaten tree trunks. Things that sometimes never turned up again.

The search had been extensive. There'd been MISSING posters attached to telephone poles and hung in store windows. Grandmother's photograph even appeared on the local news. The photo they used was one in which Amelia had also appeared. In it, the two were hugging, their wide smiles crinkling the corners of their eyes. When they showed it on TV, they'd cropped Amelia out, which hurt.

It made her feel like they'd cut off a piece of her body.

Amelia's anger had sparked a couple months ago, when she'd overheard her mothers speaking late one night after lights out. Mama had been crying in the living room, and Mom was trying to comfort her. They'd said things like, *I'm tired of this . . . Want it to be over . . . Just like my father . . . Time to move on . . . Not coming back . . .* That night they'd made the decision to sell Grandmother's house. Having strained to listen until the mothers fell asleep, Amelia lay in bed, trying to control her ragged breath, staring at the ceiling until the sun came up.

Part of wanting to take the book back to the library had been to escape the slow packing up of Grandmother's life.

Head held high, she walked by the grocery store and the lunch place and the hardware store and the Victorian inn that reminded her of the house in that movie about the family of witches who'd been cursed by an ancient ancestor. The one where the women would leap off the roof every Halloween and float gently to the ground. In the town where Grandmother had lived, many of the buildings were partially covered in creeping ivy, and at this time of year, their leaves always turned a vibrant red and flickered gently in the wind as if to say *Watch out.* Amelia thought she heard Winter whistling. She winced and turned to look for him. When the sound came again, she realized it was only a bird.

One strange thing no one ever wished to discuss was that Grandfather had gone missing a decade prior, in a similar manner. Just one day, gone. Amelia had been a baby, so she didn't remember. Back then, no one had wanted to admit that Grandfather had just *run off.* They'd said he was *not that type of man.* What type was that? Amelia often wondered.

Just like my father, Mama had said. Had she been talking about the raging creek waters? Dementia? Both? Or maybe she'd meant something completely different . . .

Something she was keeping secret . . .

Amelia comforted herself by thinking that maybe Grandmother had gone looking for Grandfather.

Maybe they were together now. Safe and sound.

Not dead. Neither of them.

Amelia refused to believe that.

A sign for the library stood beside the road. A lush green lawn rolled out before a stark white building. From here, the library looked like a small cottage. A path of stones led across the yard from the sidewalk, each one sunk deep into the grass, as if the earth were trying to devour them. Amelia hopped from stone to stone imagining that the grass was lava and if she were to trip, the earth would devour her too. She caught herself and glanced around to see if anyone was watching. *Don't*, she scolded. How would she ever join the yearbook crew next year if the kids at school mocked her for doing nonsense like this?

Grow up, Amelia . . .

Opening the library's skinny door, she realized that the building appeared to be bigger on the inside than had been noticeable from the street. Beyond the front desk, several doorways opened onto rooms filled with endless shelves stuffed with books, a long straight corridor leading to a room at the back, and two sets of stairs, one of which went up to a second floor while the other descended into shadow. Amelia felt an urge to wander, to pluck a book from a shelf, to sit and read for a good long while—long enough to forget about what Mom and Mama were doing up at the house. Was it a good idea? Her mothers would be busy for another few hours at least, and the longer Amelia kept her distance, the less likely she'd be to snap at Winter for some dumb thing or another.

At the desk, a thin woman with thick round glasses glanced up. Her black hair was streaked with gray and pulled into a short ponytail. She wore a gauzy brown dress that looked like it had been constructed from the faded floral wallpaper in Grandmother's powder room off the kitchen. A plastic card hung from a black lanyard around her neck. It read: *Mrs. Bowen, Librarian.* The woman's age seemed slippery. She might have been thirty. She might have been fifty.

Amelia approached, holding out the library book. "Excuse me," she said. The librarian's suspicious eyes were enormous behind those lenses. "I found this in my grandmother's attic." Amelia laid it on the desk. "It was due a long time ago."

The librarian picked up the book and looked at the spine. She opened the cover and saw the card in the paper pocket. "A long time ago indeed," she said, puzzled. Glancing at Amelia, she asked, "And who is your grandmother?"

"Susannah Turner." Speaking the name aloud, even at a whisper, made Amelia all tingly, as if it were a spell that might bring her back. She made a mental note to do it more often.

The librarian sighed. "I'm so sorry for your loss, honey. Oh, how we miss her here."

Amelia flinched. *What loss?* she wanted to say. "That's okay," she replied instead. "She's been gone for over a year now." The worried look on the librarian's face made her wish she'd kept that to herself, and yet, there was something satisfying about making an adult uncomfortable. "My moms are packing up the old house. Time to sell, I guess. I wish *we* could move in. Keep it for her in case she . . ." The librarian's eyes widened. This was the wrong direction to take, Amelia realized. She backtracked, "It's just, the house is so big. So much to explore."

The librarian smiled. There. Better. Grown-ups loved hearing about the curiosity of kids. "I remember. Your grandmother invited me to quite a few dinner parties. Such a lovely lady," the woman finished, as if Amelia hadn't said a word about what may or may not have been her grandmother's tragic ending. Amelia chewed at her lip. This was a hard part—the listening as other people made judgments and drew their own conclusions.

Sudden sadness brushed softly against the inside of Amelia's skull. She focused on the book again in case some of that emotion tried to find its way out. "I don't have any money to pay a fine. I just wanted you to have it back."

The librarian shook her head. "Well, that's very nice, dear, but your grandmother's book isn't from our library."

Amelia was confused. "Are you sure?" As soon as she said it, she felt her face flush.

The woman ran her finger along the embossed title. "*Tales to Keep You Up at Night*. I read this when I was your age." She shuddered, looking suddenly much older than Amelia had first thought, maybe even as old as Grandmother. "If we ever had a copy, I'd remember." Wearing a wistful squint, she handed the book back to Amelia. "Gosh, I wish I could read it again for the first time. Maybe your grandmother wanted you to have it."

A flash of the dream from the previous night. Grandmother in the attic, stepping from the shadows, holding the book out. Opening the cover. Showing Amelia something written on the first page . . . But what had it said? In her memory of the dream, the words blurred, the letters shifted, transformed, shifted back.

Amelia stared at the silver title on the spine again, imagining what was concealed between the bindings. *Tales* . . . She wasn't sure she wanted to know. She'd never ventured into these kinds of stories before. Lately, she'd been obsessed with biographies. Shirley Chisholm. Eleanor Roosevelt. The female pharaoh, Hatshepsut. Joan of Arc. And her namesake, Amelia Earhart. But if Grandmother had wanted her to read it—and Amelia *did* feel like her dream had been a visit from Grandmother, wherever she was—shouldn't she try? "Are the tales *very* creepy?" Amelia asked.

"Kept *me* up at night."

Amelia felt nervous but also curious. Did she *want* to be kept up at night? Wondering where Grandmother had gone had kept Amelia up more nights during the past year than she cared to count. She thought of how the two of them would make tea in the afternoons, steeped strongly, with lots of honey and milk. Of the walks they'd take on mornings when Amelia was lucky enough to wake up at the old house after nights filled with card games and dominoes. Of Grandmother's clothes that had been semi-stylish maybe twenty years prior, pastel cardigans and thin turtleneck sweaters and polyester pants with creases so sharp they could cut paper, her hair high and tightly curled, done at the hairdresser weekly. She thought of the house up the hill where her parents were working so diligently, and how it would soon be empty.

Amelia rubbed at her eyes. Was it possible that Grandmother had read this book? If Amelia read it too, might they be connected again? Could it be that stories stretched across the distance that separated them, however far that was?

"Is there somewhere I can sit for a while?" Amelia asked.

"Feel free to take a look."

"Thanks." Amelia hugged the book to her chest again, then strolled past the circulation desk. Without turning, the librarian lifted a hand, gave a wave, and went back to her work.

Down the corridor, Amelia found a small room with two wooden desks and a view out the rear of the library. Orange and yellow leaves turned the afternoon's sunlight into a dim, stained-glass glow that spilled onto the wide floorboards. Beside the desks, a couple of comfy-looking leather chairs sat, a coffee table between them. Amelia plopped into one of them, opened the book she'd found in Grandmother's attic, and with a deep, shaky breath, turned to the first story.

MOLL'S WELL

There are many ways a story can echo through time. For Moll Bowen, tales of her own family resonated in her mind long into her elder years, mostly as a result of a book she'd carried from the old country—a stiff, leather-bound thing whose yellowed pages would crinkle whenever she opened it. Inside were names and dates and histories going back generations. More importantly, some might argue, there were recipes for remedies and tinctures and poems (the earliest Bowens had called them spells, but Moll never spoke of such things).

Believe it or not, there once were days, years, decades, and centuries when physicians were scarce, and so folk came to depend on women and men like Moll and her family. In secret, villagers would visit the old woman's home up on Zion Hill and ask for help with love, money, and health (and sometimes, even, revenge). Moll was always happy to oblige, but for a price, of course. Though the bits of coin, slaughtered hares, pheasants, and bunches of turnips, greens, and beans were welcome, more important to Moll were words of appreciation—acknowledgment from her patrons that her skills were indispensable and unparalleled; she wanted to know that she had truly helped them, for that was what she cared most about. In this way, Moll came across as prideful, but so effective were her services, the people were more than pleased to pay her small sums and offer those slight phrases of gratitude.

The Bowens had long been known as practitioners (of a sort), and Moll had forever looked forward to passing her knowledge (her tales, remedies, and poetry) to her offspring, and to her offspring's offspring.

Little did she know, however, how drastically the circumstances in the nearby village would change before she'd have her chance . . .

There are many ways that stories can echo through a community.

Wives whisper to husbands. Children share at school. Preachers bellow to congregations. Writers publish in papers. Some folk even believe that stories can travel through dreams.

Whatever the manner, tales of the Bowens twined the area swiftly, taking hold of suspicious minds. Locals spoke of the strange family with such frequency that lore sprang up around them and their house and the nearby woods, like the water from her well that old Moll would use for her tinctures and broths. To cure a cough. To steady vision. To unbreak a heart. Moll's Well, as it came to be known, was filled with the sweetest, purest water one might wish to sip. No other natural spring in the area came close to the taste of the groundwater under Moll's property, which only added further to the legends of her cures.

Sometimes, from the window of her cottage, Moll watched the sons of prominent locals sneak to the stone structure that her own sons had dug out and constructed decades earlier. Daring one another, the young trespassers would lower her bucket and steal huge gulps, hoping the liquid would bring them extra luck. Moll never minded; she believed that if one were lucky enough to be blessed with such a gift as sweet water, one must share it. What Moll didn't expect was that the boys would bring home stories about Moll's intense stare from behind the darkened glass of her home—a look they believed was a scowl.

The people began to call her the witch of the woods. They said she had powers acquired from living close to several mysterious boulders, inventing tales that these massive alabaster rocks were remnants, crumbled from the walls of paradise, which had been blasted apart far and wide after a trickster serpent had caused the fall of Humanity. Moll felt it was a preposterous notion (to anyone with a lick of logic), but its roots dug deeper the more the story's seeds were watered. So, even though *preposterous notions* made up the bulk of Moll's daily bread, their roots began to choke away her steady stream of customers until the people who visited were few and far between.

Rumors echoed. Over time, the echoes clamored. Lore spread that the Bowens visited you in dreams and made you see things that were not there, that Moll communed with inhuman spirits of the forest, working with them to exact the magic she needed for her garden, her recipes, her words. People came to believe that even the well was magicked, either by the alabaster boulders out in the wood or by Moll's own will.

When the echo of these rumors reached Moll's own ears, she wrote to her children and grandchildren, who lived miles across the rolling hills. In her letters, she confessed fears that a change was coming, something big, and she asked if her family would venture home to help. So worried was she that she planned, on their return, to hand off her family's book of shadows—the one containing tales of the Bowen legacy, with its tincture recipes and stories and poems and family tree trunks, branches, and stems.

Her children were due to arrive on Moll's ninetieth birthday. October was her daughter. November and December were her sons. Each of them were solid of body, if not mind, but what all of them shared most strongly was a love for the woman who had raised them.

Moll spent those last few days of peace listening from behind the shuttered windows for the squeaking turns of wooden wheels and the huffing breath of horses. She went so far as to arrange a type of alarm—jingle bells attached to string tied to low saplings around her property so she'd know if anyone was approaching.

You see, earlier that week, a man had come to the village—a man who'd heard those same echoes of rumor and who was determined to do something about them.

About Moll.

The man's name was Turner, and he was known far and wide as the Judge, as the law had given him authority to mete out justice to those whom he determined deserved it.

And so, on her birthday, when Moll finally heard those wooden wheels and huffs of horses' breath, the visitors were not the ones for which she had hoped.

Bells rang out. *Jingle-jangle. Jingle-jangle.* Moll hobbled to the window.

The faces in the yard were mostly familiar to Moll except for the tall, pale man wearing the black suit and wide-brimmed hat. His eyes were piercing and dark, and at first glance, they sent waves of fright through Moll's frail frame.

This man was *the change* she'd warned her children about, she knew now.

Turner called her name, his voice booming through the woods, rustling crows from the branches, scattering them frantically into the wind cawing together like an alarm. Moll stepped out onto her stoop, taking in the crowd. The folk who used to come to her for help were now wearing darker expressions. She was tempted to acknowledge each of them by name, the Spencers, the Fullers, the Carvers, the Brewsters, the Martins, the Winslows, and the Hathornes, to let this imposing new man know of their bonds, but she worried that this would only put these people, whom she believed to be good-hearted (if only deep down) into danger.

The Judge nodded to some of the men. They seized old Moll. Then he motioned to others who pushed past her into the cottage. One emerged moments later with Moll's book in hand, raised high overhead. "Here it is!" this man shouted. "Proof of her pact with darkness!" The crowd erupted in cheers and jeers, spewing words of hate and spite and hypocrisy.

The Judge glanced through the pages, then squinted up at Moll. "Does this belong to you?" he asked.

Moll's mouth was so dry, she could barely spit out an answer. She gave a nod. "The book has long been the property of my family." She coughed, then begged the men to release her so she could drink of her well, its stones protruding from the earth, half hidden by the shadows beside her home.

The Judge shook his head. "I think not." He approached the structure that was holding her attention, and with nary a consideration, tossed Moll's book into the deep hole.

Her heart dropped a moment later as a resounding splash

echoed forth from the well's mouth.

The Bowen family's history. Their knowledge. Gone. In the wink of an eye.

"Take her," said the Judge.

As the men (whom she had once considered good neighbors) dragged the old woman down the path toward town, Moll managed to look back at the small cottage where she'd been lucky enough to raise her family.

If only they had arrived in time.

This was the last moment Moll would ever see her home. Her *true* home.

The trial was swift, Turner's judgment brutal.

Moll was to hang that very evening, from a hastily built gallows in the village square.

You may have heard of fates similar to poor Moll's. At this point in our tale, you must understand why. Stories echo through time. Sometimes stories become distorted, but sometimes they are as fresh as when they first were spoken. Since the beginning, there have been countless people in Moll's circumstances—accused, convicted, jailed, hanged, burned, forgotten—people who have been transformed into villains because, more often than not, the people who tell the stories are the ones who did the accusing, the convicting, the hanging, and the burning. The ones who lived. If these stories don't favor the accusers, then the accusers are the ones who force the forgetting.

But echoes linger in darkness. In whispers late at night from corners of bedrooms. In dusty, out-of-print volumes. In handwritten journals with cracked, yellow pages.

Later, Judge Turner may have wished that his conviction of Moll Bowen had been one of the tales that died on the wind.

As the men of the village led the old woman up the wooden steps, as torch fire made harsh light lick across her terrorized countenance, something occurred that gave rise to an enduring legend. From out of the shadows surrounding the square, a dozen or so figures stepped, holding rifles and blades that glinted in the flame. As Moll noticed her family, a grin spread her cracked lips and made them bleed. She gave the pain nary a thought; she knew she was saved.

Judge Turner tried to warn off October, November, December, as well as their spouses and their children, but the Bowens would not listen, not until the noose was removed from around the matriarch's throat and Moll was safely encircled by them.

"You dare touch our mother," a thin man with a black beard called out from the new group. He was Moll's son November. "And on the *ninetieth anniversary of her birth?*"

"What a party you all have thrown," said a solid gent, whose smile gleamed white, even as his eyes showed death. This was Moll's other son, December.

"There is no escaping judgment!" Turner bellowed as the villagers backed away from the gallows and the family perched above them, watching, as if collecting faces, collecting names. When Turner saw the villagers' fear, he changed tack and quieted. "Leave her be," he reasoned with the Bowens, "and I shall consider leniency when your own time comes to stand before me."

"You will not find her," said a tall woman in the group. Moll's daughter, October. "You will not find us."

Judge Turner spun on the villagers. "We must stop them!"

But the people of the village would no longer listen. Moll's children standing up for her had shamed the villagers, forced them to recognize their cruelty and remember the help she had offered their families over the course of her extraordinarily long life.

The Bowens edged away from the rope and to the shadows, but a moment before they would have disappeared into darkness, Moll stopped them. She faced the Judge and called out in a harsh whisper, her voice like the crunching of footsteps through brush, "May your thirst be quenched." She looked to the crowd. "May all your thirst be quenched."

As a gust of wind came whipping down the hill, the torch fires flickered nearly out, and when the light was restored, the people saw that the family was gone.

Because of the deep and sweet well, old Moll's property on Zion Hill became desired by most everyone in the area. The man who came to own the place, however, happened to be the same who had driven her from it.

Turner tore down the poor stone cottage and replaced it with a grand mansion, which he called the Manse. He moved there with his wife and children. What pleased him most was the acquisition of Moll's Well and the pure water contained in its depths.

Moll's final wish for him seemed to have come true. *May your thirst be quenched.* He never wanted for a drink another day in his life. What seems like a blessing, however, sometimes ends up a curse, especially when uttered by someone who's been wronged. Shortly after the last shingle was laid on the Manse's roof, Turner's wife found the Judge, bloated and blue, at the bottom of Moll's Well, his stomach and lungs filled to bursting with that once-sweet water.

No one knew what had happened. Had he slipped? Or had someone pushed him?

Over time, stories about the Judge's death continued to echo like voices calling from the bottom of the well. Children in the village spoke of strange happenings on the famed hill, especially after the Turners lost their fortune and abandoned the Manse, leaving it to rot and tumble down, as nature returned to Zion in the stead of old Moll, who had never been allowed. These tales did not stop the children from visiting, especially in the dead of night, when moons peaked in the sky overhead.

Years after the death of Judge Turner, a brother and sister decided to climb the hill and locate the well. They'd heard tell of curses and death, and as children are wont, they desired to see about it for themselves.

They left home when their parents were asleep. The village was more populous than before. Roads were wider so wagons could travel more efficiently. Though the brother and sister had no wagon, nor horse, under the light of the moon they made their way toward the old Bowen-Turner property. Listening to the night's cricket song and the percussive crunching of larger, furred hunters through the dry forest scrub, they paused every now and again, uncertain if something out there was listening to them too.

Finally, they found what they'd come for. The Manse's roof was bowed now, and some of the slate had slid away, showing dark holes that gaped up at the sky, as if in awe. Though the grass of the yard was tall, wavering in a weak breeze, no trees grew around the old house, as if they did not wish to spread roots through cursed soil.

The boy pointed toward the circular pile of stones a couple dozen yards from the building's foundation. The ruins of Moll's Well still stood. The tale he had heard from an uncle, who was prone to sharing things with the children he probably should not have, was that anyone who chanced glancing into the well on a bright night like this would gaze upon a reflection that was not their own.

The girl took her brother's hand, and together, they tromped through the grass, breaking stalks and leaving deep boot prints, daring the ghosts of the old place to scold them. She was the first to reach the piled stones. The edge came up to her hips. She placed her hands on the lip, but instead of peering down, she looked to her brother, who was hesitating to join her there. "Are you a fraidy-cat?" she asked.

Younger by a year, the boy was determined not to show the fear that seized him. "Shush," he whispered, mirroring his sister's stance—hands on the stones, hunched over, ready to test the veracity of Uncle's tale. The boy looked into his sister's eyes. Her wide gaze gave away her own terror.

Why did we come here? he suddenly wondered. Who would tell their story if neither of them made it home again? Right then, he wanted *more than anything* to make it home again. He'd heard that the Bowens had never left the town, that they'd only moved deeper into the forest . . . that they were the ones who'd pushed Judge Turner over the edge of *these very stones.*

What must it have felt like tumbling into darkness? Hitting limbs and scalp and skin on the walls as you went down, down, down? He'd heard that the Bowens were evil, but then he remembered what the villagers, what *the Judge* had done to the family, and he wondered who were the evil ones.

Were the Bowens really capable of magic? Could they visit your dreams? Build doorways from their house to yours simply by scribbling some arcane symbols and writing their names on the walls? Command creatures that come from other, darker realms? Attempt to live on eternally? Or were these stories made up by guilty people who wanted to control what future generations thought of the scorned family?

Were these stories merely echoes, distorted by time . . . and the tellers?

If the Bowens still lived . . . what would they feel when those echoes reached their own ears? Would they ignore them? Or might they embrace the tales, make them true somehow, as if they were capable of a new kind of revenge upon those who would corrupt their legacy?

Something splashed.

Something in the water below.

Don't look, said a voice in the boy's mind.

But then his sister began to count. "One . . . two . . ." And he knew it was too late. They were here. They had to go through with it, no matter the consequences. "Three!"

Together, they peered into the well.

At first, the boy saw nothing. But then, the far ripples quieted, and the moon, which was just overhead, solidified in the reflection. A great, glowing orb. Soon, he could see his own face, and the face of his sister staring up. It was not so different from the looking glass at his mother's bedroom vanity.

His uncle had been incorrect. There was no curse. For all the boy knew, there had been *nothing* to the story of old Moll and Judge Turner and this property and this well. Just because someone tells you a tale and says it's true doesn't make it so. He wondered: Is there a word for when you feel both disappointment and relief at the same time?

The boy was about to back away, when his sister stifled a gasp and then pressed her hand on top of his own. It was then that he saw it.

Down at the bottom of the well.

Reflected in the still water.

The dark figure rising up behind them, faceless, as it blocked out the light of the moon.

The boy tried to turn. To see. But cold fingers clutched his shoulders, ragged nails scraped his skin. There was a shove and a shift of weight, and before he could stop it, he felt himself falling forward, into the mouth of stones. He dangled there for a moment, the waist of his pants catching on a rough piece of mortar, and he waved his hands, helplessly, as he watched what was happening in the reflection below.

The figure grew taller behind him, blacker than the night sky. In one brief glint, it seemed that a smile appeared where a smile might have been. He was sure then he would learn what it was to tumble down, down, down.

But then his pants cinched. His sister yanked him back. And together they settled into the tall grass, arms wrapped around each other, as they heaved breath. Then, looking quickly around the clearing, they saw that they were alone. No dark figure was near. None that they could see anyway. If anyone had smiled at them, the boy knew now, it had been down in the depths of that hole. The Judge, he was certain, had punished them for disrespecting the place where he'd perished.

Later, after they had rushed down the hill into the village, and stumbled almost blindly back into their own yard, the boy realized that his sister had her own version of what had happened. "The witch," she whispered quietly so their parents would not wake. "She almost got us."

"It wasn't the witch," the boy argued. "There never was a witch. The person who pushed me was the Judge."

"No way it was the Judge. Why would a good man turn bad after he died?"

"Because he was never a good man?"

The siblings realized then that the argument would have no resolution. To continue on would only lead to their parents discovering them standing in the moonlight. But the question remained even as they slipped into bed: Whose face had reflected up from that dark water? The Judge? Or the witch? And which of them had tried to shove the boy down, down, down?

As they grew older, each of the siblings repeated the story of what happened that night to any child willing to listen.

Their stories echoed through generations, changing with each new teller, so that when it reached the current time, the one in which *you* live, neither of the tales could be said to be true anymore . . . as if they ever were.

As time and space can distort both echoes and stories, what is important to note is that both must begin with a voice.

Sometimes that voice sings a song, whispers a secret, chants a rhyme.

Sometimes the voice shrieks in pain. Or fear. Or joy.

Sometimes the voice accuses. Condemns. Apologizes.

Sometimes the voice (the echo) changes, and thus, the story with it.

When that voice belongs to you, be warned. For once you tell a tale, you cannot take it back. And you might be surprised by what a story, set loose in the world, can do.

AMELIA AND THE LIBRARIAN

Amelia looked up. The reading room came into focus.

Wasn't *Bowen* the librarian's last name? Just like old Moll? Amelia was certain she'd read it on the ID card hanging from the lanyard around the woman's neck.

An odd coincidence.

Amelia glanced down the hall to the empty circulation desk. *Kept* me *up at night*, Mrs. Bowen had claimed. If that were true, might it have been for more than one reason? Amelia snapped the book shut, then leaped to her feet. "Mrs. Bowen?" she called out, not too loudly, because it was a library after all, and she didn't wish to disturb anyone. She peered into the hall. A yelp made her jump, and she nearly dropped the book.

The librarian had been standing, wide-eyed, just on the other side of the doorway, by a set of stairs that led down to the basement. "You scared me," she said with a relieved laugh.

"I'm sorry. It's just, I wanted to ask you . . . Do you know who wrote this book?" Amelia held it up, ran her finger down the spine, then flipped the cover open to the front pages. "The author isn't listed."

The woman shook her head. "I'm not sure. We could look it up."

But Amelia didn't want to look it up. She wanted to ask the librarian. "I noticed the name *Turner* in this first tale. That's my grandparents' name. Grandmother's married name. It's part of my own last name. *Turner*-Ingersoll. Mom and Mama combined the two on the day they got married."

"Curious," the librarian answered, eyes squinting as if she were considering something she didn't wish Amelia to know.

Even so, Amelia wasn't sure if the woman was only humoring her. "And also, well . . . Did you know *your* name is also in this tale? 'Moll's Well'?"

The woman shook her head again, more slowly this time. "I did not."

Amelia pointed to the page. "See? Right here. *Bowen.*"

The librarian's lips popped open in surprise. "But *my* last name is *Brown.*" She grabbed at the lanyard at her neck and showed Amelia the ID card. "I suppose they're similar though, in a way. Brown. Bowen."

Amelia scrunched her brow. "I thought . . ." But did it matter what she'd thought? The librarian's face stared out from the photo on the ID, right next to her clearly printed name. Mrs. Brown. *Brown*, not *Bowen*. "I guess I misread your tag earlier. I'm sorry."

"You said the name Turner is in the book too?" Mrs. *Brown* went on, trying to smooth over any awkwardness.

"Right," Amelia answered. "Yes. He's the Judge in the first tale."

"Ahh." Mrs. Brown smiled. "I remember that one. He was the villain?" Amelia nodded. "Hope you're not actually related to him," she whispered playfully. "Wouldn't want to have *that guy* as an ancestor."

Amelia raised an eyebrow. "He's a character in a story."

"Maybe the story is true," the librarian answered mysteriously. Amelia smiled, showing that she knew Mrs. Brown was teasing. "Excuse me, but I've got business to attend to." The librarian winked and then descended the stairs.

Back in the leather chair, Amelia felt her face flush. Was it more shame about sharing a name with that nasty character? Or maybe it was about how Amelia had gone almost out of her way to wrongly connect the librarian with the story? Since Mrs. Brown *wasn't* a Bowen, maybe the book wasn't as strange as she'd first imagined.

But then, another flash of the previous night's dream popped into Amelia's head.

Grandmother in the attic.

A worried look. A twisted grimace.

She was holding the book. *Tales.* She was opening the cover.

This time, however, Amelia made out the words on the title page, written in black, scratchy pen. *DO NOT READ THIS BOOK.* She recognized Grandmother's distinctive handwriting somewhere in the warped scrawl.

She flinched. The vision was so vivid, she wondered how she could have not remembered until this very moment. Quickly, she opened the book on her lap again. To check . . . But the endpapers were blank.

The writing had only existed in the dream.

Still, it felt somehow as though it had been a message from Grandmother, from . . . *wherever* she was now. Despite the hope she insisted on holding, Amelia didn't want to think too hard about where that might be.

In the tale of Moll's Well, the Bowens had been able to visit people in dreams. Was it possible that Grandmother had done the same?

Her message had been to *not* read this book. And yet, Amelia had a feeling that in these pages there must be a clue about where Grandmother had gone. And how would she learn more unless she ignored Grandmother's request. Unless she *did* read the stories?

Of course, there was also the strong possibility that her memory of Grandmother in the attic had been *nothing more* than a dream.

Amelia thought suddenly that it was a good thing this volume of tales did not belong to the library. That the book was not overdue. That there would be no fine. This meant she could hold on to it, put it in the box with the other items she'd collected from her grandmother's house.

She'd been planning to make a scrapbook of memories. As a memento. In it would go pictures of her and Winter and Mom and Mama, and more importantly, of the fun times they had with Grandmother. Ticket stubs to movies and plays. Swatches of worn fabric from antique doll clothes. Even old grocery lists and calendar markings, written in Grandmother's own hand.

(*DO NOT READ THIS BOOK.*)

All of it would be evidence of her legacy, pieces of the family's history, like pinpoints on a timeline. (Like in old Moll's book of shadows . . .)

A year ago, just after Grandmother had gone away, when there was still hope that she'd return, and as Amelia had begun gathering these items from Grandmother's house, she'd suggested to Mr. Frasier at school that the elementary schoolers should have a yearbook, like they did for the kids in middle school and beyond. It seemed important that she document the year, because who knew what one might need to remember? *As life occurs,* Amelia had thought, *it's difficult to know what's important and what's not.* To understand what it all might add up to someday. So shouldn't one keep the keepsakes? Turn them into something worthwhile? A kind of treasure?

Mr. Frasier had agreed to help, but because they'd had no budget, the only "yearbook" that Amelia had been able to come up with was a black-and-white pamphlet, a single staple in the center of about a dozen folded pages. Scotty and Georgia had helped her put them all together. Their classmates loved how it came out. Even though the pamphlets sort of looked like a summertime arts and crafts project, she'd been proud of what they'd made.

She knew that Grandmother would have been proud of her too.

Next year would be better. With a budget. And a bigger team. And people who knew what they were doing.

The sunbeam crept across the wooden planking of the library floor. Daytime was seeping away.

Amelia recalled the dream's scrawl. *DO NOT READ THIS BOOK.* At this point, with answers at her fingertips, how could she not turn another page?

THE BABYSITTER
AND THE BELL

Jenny Carver stood on the porch of the white clapboard house. The dark roof rose in a high tower over the front door like a witch's sharp hat. Black shutters hugged the windows. Inside, heavy curtains were drawn shut.

Jenny adjusted the hem of her shirt and hiked up her jeans, which had been sagging, as usual. This was her first babysitting job, and she was determined to do everything right. She worked up the courage to ring the doorbell. Moments later, a woman opened the door. "Mrs. Frederick? Hi, I'm Jenny."

The woman smiled and stepped aside.

Mr. Frederick was coming down the large winding staircase, straightening his tie. "Welcome, Jenny," he said when he saw her. "Thanks for helping us out at the last minute."

"My pleasure," Jenny answered. To her ears, it sounded professional.

"Has she met Lucy yet?" Mr. Frederick asked his wife.

"I was just about to bring Jenny back to the den," Mrs. Frederick answered. "Lucy's watching her shows."

Jenny followed Mrs. Frederick down a long corridor with emerald-green wallpaper and a midnight-colored trim. At the rear of the house was an atrium. Giant windows were held together by black girders. Thick dark rugs covered most of the red brick floor. A tufted leather couch sat in the center, facing a wide television that was perched on a low table. A small girl was sprawled out on the rug several feet from the screen, her head resting on her hands, her feet raised behind herself, kicking carelessly at the air.

Jenny's mother had mentioned that Lucy was five years old, but the girl was smaller than Jenny's cousins, who were the same age. Lucy's black hair sprang from around her face in an explosion of tight ringlets. When she looked at Jenny, her tiny smile shone. She leaped to her feet, but then paused before running to her mother's side and clutching at her leg.

Jenny crouched down, bringing her face close to the little girl's. She held out her hand. "You must be Lucy," she said softly. "My name is Jenny. Nice to meet you." But Lucy only stared. Jenny had spent many hours with her cousins, so she knew how to handle kids. "We're going to have fun tonight. Do you like games?"

Lucy moved a step away from Mrs. Frederick's leg. Her mother kept her hand on the girl's head. "What kind of games?" Lucy asked.

"*Pretending* games," Jenny answered.

Lucy smiled again. "I like pretending." Then, as if from nowhere, she added, "I have a stuffed alligator named Messy."

Jenny held back a guffaw. "I can't wait to meet them. Will Messy play with us too?"

Wide-eyed, Lucy nodded slowly.

"You two sit and get to know each other," said Mrs. Frederick. "Daddy and I will finish getting ready. Then, you and Jenny can play all the games you like." She winked at Jenny, then left them alone. Jenny felt a warmth in her chest, happy knowing that she was already doing a great job.

Lucy tried to explain the cartoon show that she'd been watching, and Jenny listened, understanding only about half of what the girl was saying. After the Fredericks came back, they showed Jenny where the kitchen was, where to find Lucy's favorite snacks, and a list of phone numbers. They showed her Lucy's bedroom and bathroom upstairs and then gave her a rundown of Lucy's routine. "We shouldn't be back too late," said Mr. Frederick. "It's just a dinner with my boss and his husband. If you need anything, please call."

Within minutes, the couple was gone, and the place settled into a kind of quiet. Jenny let out a shallow breath she'd been holding since she'd pressed the doorbell. She was alone in a large, strange house with a little girl she didn't know in a neighborhood far from home. Safety was her responsibility.

The last of the sunlight was draining from the sky. Jenny clenched her fists, angry at herself for feeling suddenly afraid when she knew she could do this. The television echoed from the back room. She peeked through the doorway to find that Lucy was still entranced, then she went into the kitchen and examined the list of numbers the Fredericks had left on the notepad. The closest neighbors were five hundred yards down the road. An older couple called the Doughertys. There was the fire department and the local police. And she could always reach her mother at home, though that was the last thing Jenny wished to do. Her mother had trusted her to take this job by herself.

Lucy loved the games that Jenny came up with—The Huntress and the Deer, The Stone Child, Mother's Poison Garden, Evade the Laser, and Jenny's personal favorite, The Floor Is Lava. Lucy's alligator, Messy, played along, well past the hour Lucy was supposed to have brushed her teeth.

When Jenny noticed the time, she nearly screamed. What if the Fredericks came home right at this moment? She tried to get Lucy upstairs, but by that point, Lucy didn't want to go. She was on the verge of tears, when Jenny convinced her she'd been saving the absolute *best* game for when Lucy was tucked under the covers. Lucy caved, and Jenny's mind raced as the little girl used the bathroom, trying to come up with one final game that would be better than all the rest. It turned out, however, that Jenny needn't have worried, because as soon as Lucy's head hit the pillow, her eyelids started to droop.

The lamp on her side table cast a soft glow across the blankets. "Tell me a night-night story," Lucy asked blearily.

But before Jenny could start in on a story, from some distant part of the house, a bell rang. It wasn't the doorbell, nor did it sound like an alarm. It was a light tinkling sound, a single chime that reminded Lucy of the bell choir at church during Christmas.

Standing by Lucy's bedroom door, Jenny tried to get a sense of where it was coming from. At first, she was certain it was downstairs, but when she turned back to Lucy, it shifted, as if now overhead.

Lucy's eyelids fluttered nearly shut. Jenny knelt down and whispered into the girl's ear. "Do you hear that ringing?" she asked.

Lucy nodded sleepily. "It's Granny. She lives upstairs. She rings her bell when she wants a glass of water."

Chilly fingers poked Jenny's spine. "Your grandmother lives here with you? In this house?"

"*Granny*," Lucy said, nodding, her eyes completely shut now.

Jenny inhaled a shallow breath. "And she's been with us? This whole time?"

"She wants a glass of water," Lucy murmured again, her lips barely moving.

From the hall, Jenny could see where the staircase curved toward the upper level. Why wouldn't the Fredericks have told her about Granny? The ringing went on. She ran down to the kitchen, grabbed a glass from the cupboard, and filled it with water from the sink. Then, focusing on the dark at the top of the stairs, she made her way to the third floor.

On the upper landing, light leaked out from around the edges of a closed door. Up here, the ringing almost hurt Jenny's ears. As soon as she knocked, the sound stopped, and a thin voice answered, "Come in . . ."

An old woman was lying in the center of a large brass bed that was covered in mounds of patchwork quilts. A tiny crystal lamp hung from the ceiling, casting streaks and rainbows on dingy beige walls. A faded yellow curtain covered the single window in the far wall.

As Jenny stared from the doorway, the woman placed the bell onto the table beside the bed, damping its resonance. The woman sat up, her thick glasses slipping down her nose. She was dressed in a black nightgown, ratted ruffles like dead flower petals at her neckline. Her eyes were a warm brown, just like Lucy's. "Hello, dear," said the woman, glancing at the glass that trembled in Jenny's grip. "I see the other girl already told you what I needed." She reached out, her parched lips opened slightly, her dry tongue slithering just inside.

Jenny handed over the glass, then stepped back quickly, out of reach. "Mr. and Mrs. Frederick didn't tell me you were here," she said to the woman. "I'm sorry. I would have brought Lucy up to spend some time with you."

The old woman smiled. "Don't worry yourself, dear."

The night was getting stranger and stranger. "Are you hungry too? Can I get you a snack?"

The old woman shook her head. "Water is enough, thank you." She glanced at the bell on the table. "If I need anything else, I'll be sure to ring."

"Okay, then," said Jenny, stepping out onto the landing. "Good night."

"Good night, dear."

Jenny closed the door and headed downstairs. She passed by Lucy's bedroom and heard heavy breathing. The girl was fast asleep. Jenny continued down to the den where she settled onto the couch, nervous jolts rattling her bones. She wondered what Granny was doing now. Sleeping? Reading? Jenny didn't remember seeing a television up there, or even a radio.

She turned on a movie and tried to pay attention to the story, but every creak or bump, every gust of wind, every hum and click of the furnace made her wonder if there might be another person in another part of the house that the Fredericks had neglected to tell her about. Would it be rude to mention when they returned how uncomfortable this had made her feel? Would it be terrible to tell them she never wanted to come back?

Jenny's eyes were closing when she heard a car pull into the driveway. She wiped at her mouth and then sat up, turning off the television and straightening her clothes. She slapped at her cheeks, trying to force away grogginess. There was a clattering of keys as the front door opened. Footsteps entered the foyer and then came softly down the dark hall. Jenny stood and pulled up her pants, which were sagging, as usual, when the couple appeared in the doorway.

"How was she?" asked Mrs. Frederick. "No trouble, I hope."

Jenny mentioned the games they'd played and how easily Lucy had fallen asleep. Mrs. Frederick's eyes seemed glazed, but she took out her wallet and removed some cash.

Jenny couldn't hold back the question any longer. "Why didn't you tell me about Lucy's granny on the third floor?" Jenny asked.

The Fredericks flinched, then glanced at each other. "Lucy told you . . . about Granny?" asked Mr. Frederick, looking more awake than he had been moments earlier.

Jenny nodded. "Just after Granny rang the bell."

Now the Fredericks looked confused. "You *heard* the bell?" asked Mrs. Frederick.

"I went upstairs, and Granny asked for a glass of water," Jenny added. "She seemed very nice, but . . . I just wish you had told me that we weren't alone in the house."

"Did Lucy put you up to this?" Mr. Frederick asked with a strained chuckle.

"Of course not," Jenny said.

Mrs. Frederick sniffed, looking annoyed. "It's getting late. I should drive you home."

Why were they acting like this? "What if there had been a fire?"

"That's enough," said Mrs. Frederick sharply. "No one is in the attic. Lucy's grandparents live elsewhere. Of course we would have told you if they were staying with us."

"Lucy has an imaginary friend," Mr. Frederick went on. "She says Granny lives upstairs and is always ringing a bell."

Jenny shook her head. "She isn't imaginary. I brought her a glass of water myself. She's up there right now. Lying in a big old bed and covered with blankets!"

Mr. Frederick looked amused, still convinced Jenny was playing some kind of prank. But when he saw Jenny's trembling lip, he grew pale. His face went slack, then he ran toward the foyer. Mrs. Frederick followed. Jenny crept up the stairs and waited outside Lucy's bedroom. The little girl's soft snoring echoed out into the hall.

Jenny listened to the Fredericks' footfalls on the third floor. She wondered if she should gather Lucy up from her slumber and take her downstairs.

But there was no shouting. No commotion.

The Fredericks came back. Alone. Their expressions were grim. Mr. Frederick carried the glass that Jenny had brought to the old woman. It was empty. "This was on the floor."

Jenny began, "But—"

"No one is up there." His voice was forceful. Angry.

"Have you ever sleepwalked, honey?" Mrs. Frederick asked. "If Lucy told you about Granny, maybe you dozed off while waiting for us. Maybe you *dreamed* her."

Jenny was tired of arguing. "Yes, Mrs. Frederick. That's probably what happened. I'm sorry for the confusion."

Fifteen minutes later, Jenny walked up the driveway at her house, cash tucked in her back pocket. Her mother was sitting at the kitchen table reading a magazine. "You survived!" she said.

Jenny forced a smile. She didn't mention the ringing bell or the old woman she'd seen in Lucy's attic. All she wanted to do was get in bed and forget the whole thing.

For the next few hours, Jenny wriggled around under her heavy blankets, unable to find a comfortable position. Sleep remained out of reach. Granny's face was lodged in Jenny's brain, and every time she closed her eyes, the old woman's smile grew a little bit wider.

Sometime after three o'clock, a noise echoed from the hallway. Jenny sat up, her chest tightening. It came again.

The bell. *Granny's* bell.

Ring-rinnng.

No, Jenny told herself. Maybe it was the dishwasher signaling the end of the rinse cycle. Or wind chimes on the neighbors' porch.

Ring-rinnng.

Jenny turned on her bedroom lamp. She stood up so force-fully, her heels pounded against the floor. Out in the hallway, she switched on the overhead light. "Mom?" she called. But her mother didn't answer.

Ring-rinnng.

Taking a few steps toward her mother's bedroom door, Jenny realized that the corridor looked different. Usually, the banister ended at the wall, but now it continued into a space that had never been there before. The hallway followed the banister around a sharp bend, and another set of stairs appeared.

"I'm dreaming," she told herself. "Mrs. Frederick was right."

Ring-rinnng.

Jenny looked up the new stairs. A faint glow bled from the darkness. *Don't go up there,* she thought. But the bell called again, louder now, and her feet wouldn't listen. When she reached the top, she found the same doorway she'd seen at the Fredericks' house. Light leaked out from around its edges.

The ringing went on.

Jenny opened the door.

The old woman was lying in the same brass bed under-neath mounds of those patchwork quilts. The same crys-tal lamp hung from the ceiling, casting the same streaks and rainbows on the same dingy beige walls. The faded yellow curtain covered the same single window. The woman sat up, her thick glasses perched on the crook of her long nose.

"What took you so long, dear?" the woman asked, an edge slicing her voice.

"I thought I was dreaming," Jenny said, feeling tiny, as if she were answering a teacher after getting caught passing a note in class. "This room . . . It doesn't exist."

"That's neither here nor there." The old woman's eyes darkened. "I was impressed with what a good job you did at Lucy's house. I've decided that *you* shall bring my water."

Jenny felt the room sway, and for a second, it seemed as though she were staring into a bottomless pool of shadow. "B-but—"

"Tut-tut," said the old woman. Snapping back into focus, she waved her bony fingers at Jenny. Her smile widened. "*You're* my girl now. The best girl for this job." The woman's lips parted, and Jenny caught a glimpse of sharp teeth. "Hurry, hurry," the old woman whispered, waving Jenny back downstairs. "Granny is thirsty."

THE RIDE

Ephraim Winslow was finishing an afternoon snack of cheese and apple slices when he heard the car horn—a long, almost violent-sounding beep.

He groaned. Mr. Eubanks was ten minutes early. After rushing straight home from the bus stop, ten minutes was the difference between Ephraim being nowhere-near-ready and raring-to go.

He tossed his plate onto the counter with a clatter. His mom would scold him later, and maybe his dad would call to scold him too, but he didn't care. He grabbed his swim bag from off his bed, then without even tying his shoes, he shouted goodbye to his mom, raced out the door, and dashed to the car idling at the curb.

Climbing inside and fastening his seat belt, he said, "Sorry to keep you waiting."

His teammate, Justine Gerard, wouldn't look at him. Up front, his other teammate, Caroline, ignored him too. Her father, Mr. Eubanks, slammed his foot on the gas pedal. The Pontiac peeled forward, swerving onto the road, and raced down the hill toward the intersection with the flashing red light. Panicked, Ephraim gripped the handle over the door.

Once, when Justine's mother was the carpool driver, Ephraim had watched in horror as a stray dog ran along the curb. He'd shouted for Mrs. Gerard to *WATCH OUT*. She'd hit the brakes so hard, everyone's swim bags flew off the seats. At the sound of the screeching tires, the dog had dashed away from the street, safe and sound, and barked as Mrs. Gerard geared forward. "*I'll* do the driving," she'd scolded Ephraim. "*You* do the sitting!" Since then, he'd kept his mouth shut while riding in someone else's car, but this felt like an exception.

Ephraim leaned forward slightly. "Can you slow down, please?"

Thankfully, no other vehicles were at the intersection when Mr. Eubanks flew through it.

"Mr. Eubanks?" Ephraim was used to Mr. Eubanks being untalkative—some dads were like that—but it was unlike the man to ignore Ephraim completely. Ephraim's own father didn't often get a chance to drive the carpool, not since he'd moved out, but Ephraim was sure that if Justine or Caroline were to have asked him a question, his dad would definitely have answered.

Mr. Eubanks took the next curve so quickly, Ephraim worried they might swipe the guardrail. "Slow down!" he cried out. The engine roared as Mr. Eubanks gunned the gas. Ephraim pressed himself into the seat and clutched the safety strap across his chest, just like his mom would have insisted.

Beside him, Justine wasn't wearing her seat belt. She stared forward. With every turn, she flopped over slightly, then straightened again. Her eyes never blinked. *Maybe she's as terrified as me*, he thought.

He *hoped*.

The Pontiac bumped over the bridge spanning Blackstone Creek. It zoomed faster than Ephraim's heart along the stretch of road where the fields of corn were planted in infinite rows. They passed the dairy farm and the farm stand and the shopping center and the corporate office park. There hadn't been another car on the road, or even any people, he realized. Usually, their carpool encountered traffic, crossing guards, and pedestrians. Today, it was as if the town had been emptied out.

At the next intersection, Mr. Eubanks careened through the parking lot of the Gas 'N Go and *ka-thunked* out onto the adjacent street, just barely missing the concrete and steel columns that were meant to protect the pumps. Ephraim was appalled. "Mr. Eubanks!" Mr. Eubanks cut the next turn short too, riding over the lawn of the big house on the corner. The safety belt kept Ephraim from tumbling over onto Justine, who was leaning hard against the car door. "Why are you doing this?" he cried out uselessly. The engine whined like a whipped horse.

They barreled toward a railroad crossing. As the Pontiac turned onto the tracks, Ephraim thought, *Please, no!* The wheels rocked over the ties. The car shuddered and squealed. So did Ephraim. Ahead, the tracks led into a dense tunnel of trees. *Please, please, please,* he prayed, hoping the tracks were as empty as the rest of the town.

Next thing Ephraim knew, the car had swerved out onto another road—one he didn't recognize. They passed a street sign. He swiveled to read it. Hardscrabble Road.

Where is this?

A seed of laughter was burbling in Ephraim's belly, sort of like on the night last year when his father and mother had sat him down and explained that they weren't going to be married anymore. His father had taken an apartment closer to the city, and Ephraim would have two bedrooms, two toothbrushes, two video game consoles. During the conversation, he'd started laughing and couldn't stop. Not as his parents stared with concern, then patted his hand, then got him some warm milk. Not after he'd climbed in bed and pulled the covers up to his chin. Not when his mother came to check on him. She'd asked how he was feeling. He'd guffawed weakly, tears streaming down his cheeks. Waking the next morning, he'd been unable to understand what had happened to him. It was like a possession—as if something had taken over his body and his mind and had forced him to watch from a dark corner as it reveled with uncontrolled glee.

The car squealed around another corner. The trees here were packed densely, their arms arching overhead and meeting in the middle. The car hit a pothole. A wheel crunched a large stone and some fallen branches.

Justine slumped forward. She slid down and crumpled into the space behind the driver's seat. Ephraim whispered, "Justine . . ." He tried to help her up, but his fingers sank into her skin, like clay, and he recoiled. In front, Caroline's neck was tilted at an odd angle. Soon, her head had bowed so deeply that her ear was pressing into her shoulder.

"Stop the car! Let me out!"

The driver paid no attention. Ephraim grabbed for the man's shirt, but his hand slid through it as if it were smoke. Yelping back, he caught a glimpse of the mess on the floor beside him. Justine was just a pile of gooey clothes now. And ahead, Caroline's skull was flattening, misshaping like a leaky balloon. He held back a screech.

The world outside was colored wax smeared on paper. If Ephraim were to leap out of the car, he might end up looking like Justine on the floor, only on the side of the road. Would it be better to take his chances?

Mr. Eubanks drove faster still. The velocity shoved Ephraim against the rear seat.

It was nearly impossible to reach out and seize the door handle. He yanked hard, but the door wouldn't budge.

The road became dirt. They thumped and bumped as leafy branches whacked at the sides of the car, scratching at the windows.

Ahead, the foliage opened, showing the sky. The street ended at a sharp drop-off. A deep ravine had bitten into the earth. Rockslides and gullies appeared across the way, deep divots and washouts pointing down, down, down. At first, Ephraim couldn't see the bottom, but then they went over the edge, and it appeared. A wall of trees and rocks and earth rose up toward them. He undid his seat belt and then ducked behind Caroline's seat. He put his head between his legs and covered himself with his arms, squeezing his eyes shut.

He felt weightless.

The car was flying.

Falling.

A strange sound escaped Ephraim's throat. Was it panicked laughter, same as that awful night his father left home?

Then, the car bounced, just slightly, and the next thing he knew was stillness.

There had been no crunch. No explosion. No ball of fire. The car was stopped in front of the YMCA. The parking lot was empty. No people were near, just like in the town.

Ephraim glanced around. Justine was gone. So was Caroline. The driver appeared now to be only a blurred shadow behind the wheel. The sky was darkening as it usually did at this time of day, at this time of year. December.

Ephraim opened the door and fell to the sidewalk. Pain shocked the palm of one hand, the knuckles of the other. Yanking the strap of his swim bag, he pulled it off the seat. Clambering away from the car, he kept his eyes fixed on the entry to the Y. The Pontiac's engine revved. Ephraim looked back. A thick cloud of black smoke burped from the exhaust pipe. Then, every door of the car swung open. He barreled into the building, leaving red marks on the door handles and the glass. "Help!" he shrieked.

His teammates were checking in at the front desk. Chatting parents stood in clumps, catching up, making plans, arguing about who would race in the relays during the next meet.

Ephraim swayed on his feet and then dropped his swim bag. Glancing out the front doors, he noticed Mr. Eubanks's car was gone. But a wisp of black smoke lingered where it sat a moment ago.

"Ephraim?" said a voice behind him. Justine rested a hand on his shoulder. "Where have you been?" He flinched away, remembering how his fingers had sunk into her flesh. Justine's eyes were wide and filled with shock. Caroline appeared beside her, mouth open in fright. For a moment, he wondered if the girls had come to drag him back outside.

The lobby went crooked, the floor sloping sharply. Ephraim felt himself falling, but Caroline caught his arm and eased him down. "Coach Weingarten!" she called out. "Help!"

Twenty minutes later, Ephraim was lying in the coach's office. His parents were both there, whispering with the Y's manager and Coach Weingarten, as well as a couple detectives. He couldn't comprehend what they were telling him.

He'd been missing for three days.

"On the afternoon you disappeared," said Mrs. Winslow, "you'd gone outside early. About ten minutes later, Justine rang the doorbell and asked if you were ready, and I realized something was wrong."

Ephraim felt weightless again, as if he were still falling into that ravine, as if he were sitting in the living room with his parents staring at him worriedly as he laughed and laughed. "It's not possible," he insisted. "I—I only got in Mr. Eubanks's car, like, *an hour ago*. Call him. Ask him. Ask Caroline. Ask Justine."

"You've been gone a long time," said his father, shaking his head. "Mr. Eubanks and the girls say they never saw you. Not until this afternoon. Here at the Y."

His parents brought him to the doctor. All the tests came back normal.

"It would be best if Ephraim stays home for a few days," said the doctor. "For some rest."

Ephraim couldn't argue. "If I do go anywhere, I think I'd like to walk, just for now."

When you're a kid, your whole *life* is a ride in someone else's car.

At night, the ride to swim practice replayed in his head like a horror movie he couldn't turn off.

Ephraim needed to think about other things, so he begged his mom to let him go back to school.

He rode the bus. In class, he listened to the lessons. He turned in his homework. He did this again and again.

The nightmares dimmed.

When they stopped, Ephraim asked if he could return to practice.

The parents started up the carpool again. Some days, Mrs. Winslow drove. Other days, the driver was Justine's mom. Mr. Eubanks agreed that it would be best if he sat out the rotation for a while.

On the Tuesday after Thanksgiving, Ephraim was finishing the last of his apple slices when he heard Mr. Eubanks's horn. The long *BEEEEEEEEEEEEEP* was like a sharp punch to his sternum.

He stood. The floor went wobbly. Looking out the window, he saw the maroon Pontiac at the curb. Caroline sat in the front passenger seat. Justine was in back.

The dark shadow sat behind the wheel. Ephraim could see now that it wasn't Mr. Eubanks. It was someone else.

A seed of laughter burbled in Ephraim's belly.

The girls gazed out at him, their expressions cold and blank.

"Mom!" he called. "MOM!"

Mrs. Winslow came running. "What is it?" she asked, rattled.

He pointed to the street, but the car was gone.

Only a cloud of black smoke remained, lingering in the still afternoon air. It twisted and turned and then faded away.

GREEN BEANS

Before Lloyd's visit to his great-aunt LaRue's house, his cousins had warned, "Be careful with her. She's a mean one." But by halfway through the first day, Lloyd had decided Auntie LaRue wasn't mean at all!

In the morning, she had taken him to McDonald's for an Egg McMuffin and a hash brown bar, and then later, she went back to the counter and got him one of those too-hot but extra-yummy apple pies that come in a folded cardboard sleeve. She'd let him run around at the indoor playground and had waved and smiled when he'd climbed up inside the bobblehead of Mayor McCheese. She hadn't even forced him to leave before he was ready, like Mama always did, but sat on the sidelines looking up from her paperback novel every few minutes to make sure he hadn't landed on his noggin.

Mama had told Lloyd that Auntie LaRue had been married to Grandpa Thackery's brother, Uncle Howard. And when Uncle Howard died, Auntie LaRue stayed in their old ranch house at the end of the cul-de-sac a few towns over. Lloyd's favorite thing about Auntie LaRue's was the enormous brick fireplace that separated the house in two and rose up above the roof like Humpty Dumpty's wall. Lloyd had been there several times, but he'd never stayed overnight and never by himself.

When Mama had dropped him off that morning, he had overheard her tell Auntie LaRue that Lloyd could be stubborn and to not give in to his tantrums. Lloyd agreed that he could be stubborn, but he didn't like that his mama was going around telling people about it. Auntie LaRue's response? "I know how to handle bad little boys." Lloyd had thought it was a funny thing to say. He wasn't *that* little. He'd made it to first grade, after all. He wasn't even that bad! Sure, sometimes his teacher made him stay on the special chair against the back wall, but that was only when he talked back or wouldn't sit still or finger-punted a paper football at his tablemates to make them laugh. But that was all!

There were a few clues about what was to come.

When Auntie LaRue asked him to wash his hands after the playground, and he'd only rinsed them, she sent him into the boys' room to scrub them again. And on the ride back to her house, he'd slipped out of the shoulder strap because it was pinching his neck. Auntie LaRue pulled over until he'd made it right. And then, before dinner, around the time when

Mama usually let him watch his cartoons, Auntie LaRue told him that he could read a book instead. Lloyd hated reading, so he sat on the couch in the living room with his arms folded and scowled at the fireplace. He'd even tried to explain to his great-aunt that Mama said *it was okay*, but she told him, "Not in my house, it isn't."

Maybe it was this that made Lloyd do what he did at the dinner table, or maybe it was the dinner itself. Either way, by evening, Lloyd finally understood his cousins' warning. It turned out, Auntie LaRue *was* actually mean.

The meat loaf was all right. He finished that part easily. The rice pilaf was kind of good. Buttery and salty. Also, he liked to bite the pilaf pieces into smaller and smaller segments between his front teeth.

Then there were the green beans. A large pile of soggy, almost gray, straight-from-the-can-to-the-microwave mush. Auntie LaRue ate hers right up, but when she noticed Lloyd hadn't touched his, she asked, "Don't like vegetables?" He crossed his arms again and shook his head. "If you don't eat your green beans, you can't have ice cream."

"I don't like ice cream." The lie almost hurt to say it.

"Really? I've never met a little boy who doesn't like ice cream."

"I'm not a little boy!" Lloyd yelled. Instantly, he knew it was a mistake. Auntie LaRue's eyes went wide before they got small and squinty.

"Watch your tone with me, Mr. *Lloyd*. I do not suffer fools."

"I'm not a fool!" Lloyd heard himself shout back.

Using her fork, Auntie LaRue pointed at Lloyd's plate. "You'll finish those green beans before you get up from this table."

"I won't!"

Auntie LaRue chortled. "Wanna bet?"

"How much?" Lloyd dared to answer.

His great-aunt said nothing as she rose and began to clear the table. When Lloyd stood, she shot him a glare that knocked him off his feet.

"You'll finish those green beans before you get up from this table," she said again.

"What if I *can't* finish them?"

A strange smile came upon the old woman. She knelt down next to him and looked him in the eye. "You'll still be sitting here in the dark, in the night, when the man with the upside-down head comes out looking for food."

Lloyd's spine went rigid. "The man with *the what*?"

She wore a look of satisfaction. "The man with the upside-down head. He lives in the chimney. And he slithers out every night. I always lock my bedroom door so he can't find me. But go ahead and sit here with your green beans. I'm sure you'll be *fine*."

"You're making that up," said Lloyd.

"Am I?"

Lloyd decided that she was. He could play this game. He knew how grown-ups were when they wanted you to do something you didn't want to do. He rolled his eyes. "Fine with me."

"Me too," said Auntie LaRue, arms full of serving bowls and silverware. She slipped quietly into the kitchen and loaded the dishwasher, humming a song Lloyd didn't recognize. He sat at the table, his vision blurry with anger, and stared at the gray-green mush at the edge of his plate.

Auntie LaRue came back a few minutes later and stood in the doorway. She held two ice-cream cones. Chocolate and strawberry. Double-stacked. Lloyd's favorite flavors. At first, he'd thought she'd changed her mind—that the kind woman who'd taken him to McDonald's and let him play on the playground had returned. But she only stared at him, licking at *both* of the cones. "How are those green beans looking now?"

"Gross," Lloyd said with a grunt.

"You know, the colder they get, the worse they taste."

"I don't care," said Lloyd, refusing to look at her anymore.

"I'll be in the den watching my shows if you change your mind. Maybe there'll still be some ice cream left if you finish in the next ten minutes."

"I'm not going to."

"Suit yourself," said Auntie LaRue, sounding like she was singing a nursery rhyme.

An hour went by. Maybe two. The television chattered softly down the hallway. Lloyd couldn't believe she hadn't yet come to get him. Mama would have given in a long time ago. His bottom hurt. And his legs were cramping up. The green beans on the dinner plate didn't even look like green beans anymore. They looked like something a farmer would serve to pigs. Like something you'd find at the rear of the school cafeteria's refrigerator that hadn't been touched for years. Toxic. Radioactive.

Finally, Auntie LaRue came back. When she saw the green beans were still on Lloyd's plate, she shook her head. "It's really too bad. I was beginning to like you, Lloyd."

"*What's* too bad?" he asked.

"That I won't see you again. Once the man with the upside-down head finds you out here . . . that'll be it."

"It?"

Auntie LaRue nodded simply. "*It*. I'd wish you a good night, but I already know what's coming, and well . . . it's anything but good." She flicked the light switch. The dining room was cast into shadow, a soft orange glow spilling through the kitchen doorway from the night-light next to the sink.

"Wait!" Lloyd called out. He didn't like the dark.

Auntie LaRue was a silhouette now. "You're going to eat those beans?" There was something in her voice that made it sound like she thought she'd won. Lloyd decided suddenly that the darkness didn't seem that bad.

"No," he answered. "I just wanted to say thank you for dinner."

"Hmph," said Auntie LaRue. "Don't try to throw them away, or put them in the garbage disposal or flush them down the toilet. *I will know*." She disappeared around the corner.

She'll be back, he told himself as the shadows crept closer. *She's just testing me*. From down the hall there came a click as Auntie LaRue shut her door and turned the lock.

Lloyd steamed.

She'll be back.

The next thing Lloyd knew was his face pressed up against the cold table, slobber coating his cheek.

He sat up in the stiff chair, wondering briefly where he was. Then it hit him. It was the middle of the night. Auntie LaRue hadn't been playing a game. Or if she *had* been playing, clearly Lloyd had lost.

All of his anger came rushing back. When his mama arrived in the morning, he'd tell her all about this. Maybe they'd even call the police. Heck, he could do it himself. He pushed the chair away from the table and wandered into the kitchen. The night-light was still beaming next to the sink. He grabbed the phone off the cradle and was about to dial the number for emergencies when he heard the noise coming from the earpiece. It wasn't the soft tone he'd expected, but the harsh *EEP-EEP-EEP* of a line that was off the hook.

I'll go lie down, Lloyd thought. *Auntie LaRue will never know.* He tiptoed toward the hall, but as he passed the living room, something echoed in the fireplace. It sounded like bits of gravel or dirt spilling down the chimney. He thought of how Auntie LaRue had tried to scare him with the tale of the man with the upside-down head. It was probably just a bird. *She knew I'd hear noises,* he thought. He continued toward the room directly across from Auntie LaRue's door, where he'd left his overnight bag. He'd have to be especially quiet so he wouldn't wake her.

Something slammed onto the living room's floor.

Wham!

Lloyd jolted, then raced down the hall, barely holding back a scream. He grabbed for the knob to the guest room, but it slipped through his sweaty palm.

There was a growling at the end of the hallway.

Lloyd's skin suddenly felt three sizes too small, and his bladder ached from the apple juice he'd had at dinner. He tried his great-aunt's doorknob instead. It was locked. He pounded on the door until his palms were numb. "Auntie LaRue!" he called out. "Help!" The only thing he could hear from the other side of the door was a clock, ticking.

The thing at the end of the hallway skittered closer. Lloyd couldn't make out what it looked like, but he could see that it was moving low to the ground. "Auntie LaRue! I'm sorry! Please!" It was closer now. Too close. Lloyd swiped at the walls, searching for a light switch. There was a pitter-pattering as the thing's appendages moved swiftly against the thick carpet. His palm met the switch. The light shone from overhead.

The thing on the floor hissed. Lloyd threw himself against the far wall, hollering for the whole neighborhood to hear. This was no lizard. No snake. It was human, or human-shaped at least. Dressed in a dark formal suit, it appeared to be walking on all fours, but its knees faced upward, along with its torso, and its elbows knocked out awkwardly as its fingers pointed at the walls. Worst of all, its head was all topsy-turvy. Its chin, which in this position should have been directed at the ceiling, was focused downward. Its head was in fact *upside-down*. Its pale skin was coated with soot. Dark hair hung down over the forehead, just barely covering eyes that were all black like a shark's.

Keeping Lloyd in sight, the creature straightened its knees, unrolled its spine, shoulders, and neck, until it was standing up. It turned around to face him. Lloyd was shocked to see that it was wearing a tattered white dress shirt and a wide purple paisley-patterned tie. The thing's mouth, which was now above its nose, which was over its eyes, widened into a grin. Small nuggets of yellow teeth looked as though they'd been pressed down into red, swollen gums.

Lloyd bolted for the guest room door again, but the man with the upside-down head tackled Lloyd to the floor, the face hovering several inches away. "Auntie LaRue!"

Breath misted out of the thing's wide mouth as it emitted a long, low *haaaaaah*. Hot saliva drooled out onto Lloyd's forehead. He could see into the thing's throat, lined with rows of those stubby teeth.

"N-nooo!" he cried.

Where was his great-aunt? How could she not hear what was happening just outside her door? Unless she wanted this to happen. Unless this was her plan.

Be careful, his cousins had said. *She's a mean one.*

Maybe Lloyd could be mean too.

"Y-you want food?" he forced himself to say. "It's really yummy." He shuddered. "F-from last night's dinner."

The thing froze, its black eyes peering into his own. It knew the word *food*. It knew the word *dinner*.

Feeling more confident, Lloyd added, "Let me up, and I'll give it to you."

The man with the upside-down head hesitated and then backed off. It slid to the side as Lloyd climbed to his feet. He eased down the hallway, not taking his eyes off of the crouching creature. When he reached the dining room, he flipped that light switch too. He rushed over and held up the plate. "You like green beans?" They were a pile of slime now, more disgusting than ever.

The man with the upside-down head angled its chin at the ceiling in contemplation, and then reached out both arms in a jerking movement, grabbing the plate away, tilting it toward its mouth. In a blink, the beans slid into its maw. The plate smashed against the floor. The man chewed, greenish juice sluicing down its face, into its upturned nostrils and wide-open, glossy black eyes.

"You *do* like green beans," Lloyd whispered.

It belched and wiped at its face with the sleeve of its suit jacket, then backed into the darkened hall, watching him all the way. Lloyd didn't move. He listened as a scrabbling sound came from the living room, claws clutching at brick. He imagined the thing climbing back up into its lair.

He waited a long time before he peered around the corner to check.

The living room was empty.

The man with the upside-down head was gone.

Lloyd woke in the morning in the guest room. Sunlight streamed in through the window. He scrambled up against the headboard, unsure how he'd gotten there. The last he remembered was staring at the darkness of the fireplace, waiting to see if the monster would come down again.

Had it been a dream?

Lloyd slipped out of bed. He was dressed in his Spider-Man pajamas, which he didn't remember putting on. He crept to the door. Sounds of cooking echoed from the kitchen, and the smell of bacon wafted in.

Lloyd edged down the hall. He didn't know what he might find beyond the kitchen entry. But it was only his great-aunt dressed in her yellow morning coat, poking at curled meat in the frying pan. "Sleep well?"

"I—I think so?" Lloyd answered.

"I guess you must have finished those green beans after all," she said, still not looking at him.

"Mm," he grunted.

When she turned, she wore thick glasses and a prim smile. "I'm glad. Did you end up loving them?" Lloyd nodded, nervous to answer in case she knew he was lying. "Have a seat. I'm assuming you like bacon, eggs, and toast."

Lloyd imagined what she wasn't saying: *Do we have to get the man with the upside-down head involved again?*

"I'll eat whatever you make, Auntie. You're an amazing cook."

"Why, thank you, Lloyd!" They sat together at the table.

He noticed that the smashed plate from the previous night had been cleaned up.

"Next time you come to visit, I'll have to teach you my tricks."

Did tricks mean recipes? he wondered. Or was she talking about something else?

Even though Lloyd wasn't hungry, he ate every last bite.

Later, when his mama came to pick him up, she asked Auntie LaRue how Lloyd had behaved. "Didn't give you too much trouble, I hope."

"Not one bit," the old woman answered. "In fact, Lloyd might have been the most entertaining guest I've ever had." She glanced at him. "Didn't we have fun, Lloyd?"

"I don't know," Lloyd mumbled. He'd already stepped toward his mother's hip, peering out from behind her.

"Sure, you do." Auntie LaRue smiled as she added, "He just adored my green beans." There was a mystery hidden in her smile—a darkness Lloyd was certain his mama could not see, a shadow that dared him to defy her. He understood even more what his cousins had meant. *She's a mean one.* Had she introduced *them* to the man with the upside-down head too? "You'd eat 'em up again tonight. Wouldn't you, Lloyd?" Auntie LaRue didn't wait for an answer before turning to his mama, her voice a hush, "I must give you my recipe."

AMELIA IN THE READING ROOM

Somewhere, a bell was ringing.

Amelia glanced up from the book, goose bumps clinging to her skin. As soon as she focused on it, the sound faded away. Had she imagined it, that chime of the woman in the attic asking for her nightly glass of water?

A car horn honked outside. An engine revved. She caught a whiff of exhaust. Amelia thought of the swirl of black smoke that Ephraim had seen lingering near the curb, like how these stories were lingering in Amelia's imagination. She zipped up her jacket.

Sunlight was still streaming through the windows in the back room where she was sitting, but now the beams stretched longer across the floor. Were her mothers wondering what was taking so long?

Amelia was about to turn the page to the next story when she noticed a brick fireplace across the room. Had it been there when she'd first sat down? She must have not seen it before. Something thumped from up inside the chimney. She held her breath, imagining the man with the upside-down head. After a moment, she figured it was probably a critter of some kind. A squirrel maybe. Or a bird.

The boy in that last story made her think of her brother. Had Lloyd gotten what he deserved? Or was Auntie LaRue the villain? Amelia grabbed at her hair and put the ends of it in her mouth, like she was wetting a paintbrush. Mrs. Jenkins would have scolded her for doing this at school, but Amelia wasn't at school right now. She could do what she wanted.

Keep going, she told herself.

SWAMP GAS

In mid-October, a nor'easter blew through Willa's town and stripped away almost all the leaves. The foliage that remained made the trees look straggly and sad, and it made Willa sad too. Willa loved scary stories. So did all of her friends. She'd been planning a spooky sleepover for months (the third in three years), and she'd hoped, as the sun descended on the upcoming party, that the surrounding hills would be a paint-splattered canvas on which to draw their scenes. Yellows, oranges, and, most importantly, reds.

Now, as the wild storm clouds lingered, everything looked gray, as if winter had arrived early, freezing out the most special of holidays.

"I don't see what the big deal is," said Willa's older sister, Issa, at lunch the day of the gathering. "No one can see the trees after dark anyway. Just use your imagination. You're already so good at that."

Willa crossed her arms and harrumphed. "It's *supposed* to be the scary season."

Willa's mother went to the window. "What better way to welcome it in than with a storm? That's pretty Halloween-y." When Willa didn't smile, she added, "Come on, now. I just said *weenie!* Chin up. Your friends will be here in a few hours."

Frustrated, Willa cleaned her plate, then went up to her room and took out some colored construction paper and scissors. When she taped the paper leaves to the wood-paneled walls in the basement rec room, Willa had to admit that her leaves (which were dotted among the old couches, bookshelves, TV, lamps that had belonged to the grandparents, some thrift store tables, and the brown shag carpet large enough to fit at least six sleeping bags) looked *slightly* magical.

Willa's mother made sugar cookies shaped like pumpkins, frosted them orange, and placed them on a plate in the center of the coffee table. By the time the first of her friends arrived, the frustration that had been broiling her brain all afternoon had evaporated. And when all the girls filled the couches, laughing and ribbing one another and dropping crumbs all over the rug, Willa stopped thinking about the storm. No one mentioned the decorations. Maybe Issa had been right. The leaves didn't matter. The *stories* did.

Willa wondered which of the girls would tell the one that kept them up till dawn. Would it be Gray, whose yarn last year had frightened their friend Denise so badly, she had to call her mom to pick her up at midnight? (Denise hadn't returned this year.) What about Charlotte? Or Peggy? They were perpetually creative. Maybe it would be Sally, who always brought a story that ended with a jump scare . . . *Boo!* Or what about the new girl, Martha, who had moved into town at the end of the summer and who everyone was still getting to know?

"Thank you for inviting me," Martha said to Willa. "It's such a great idea. I love autumn. After all, my mother's first name is October."

Willa's jaw dropped. "Is it really?" Martha nodded. *October* was one of the coolest names Willa had ever heard. "How unusual."

"It's been in my family for generations. If I ever have a kid, I'll probably name them October too."

Willa sensed they might become true friends. "I'm really happy you could come," she responded with a smile.

After the pizza showed up, Willa put on the scary movie that Gray had brought along. It didn't do much for Willa—heavy on gore and low on . . . well, everything else. Finally, it was dark enough to unroll their sleeping bags and huddle in a circle. After picking names from a wool cap that Willa had pulled from a box in the storage closet, the girls began their tales.

"Jenny Carver stood on the porch of the white clapboard house," said Sally. "The dark roof rose in a high tower over the front door like a witch's sharp hat. Black shutters hugged the windows. Inside, heavy curtains were drawn shut . . ."

Willa liked it, but where was the *jump*?

Charlotte went next. "Ephraim Winslow was finishing an afternoon snack of cheese and apple slices when he heard the car horn—a long, almost violent-sounding beep . . ."

That one left Willa feeling chilled. What was it supposed to have meant?

Peggy looked spooked before she even opened her mouth. "Before Lloyd's visit to his great-aunt LaRue's house, his cousins had warned, 'Be careful with her. She's a mean one.'"

Willa had to admit: That one was *sick*. The man with the upside-down head? Later, she'd have to put him in her journal where she kept notes about all the things that creeped her out.

Soon, there were only two names left. Willa reached into the hat and removed one slip of paper. On it was her own. Martha, the new girl, smiled from across the circle—hopefully, her story would be good, since she'd be last.

"A mother, a father, and two daughters moved into a house," Willa began, keeping her voice low and slow, watching as the girls leaned closer.

"Wait!" said Gray. "This isn't going to be one of those stories-within-a-story, is it? Those are so annoying."

Willa rolled her eyes. "Just listen, would you?" She breathed deeply, trying to settle back into the eerie mood. "A mother, a father, and two daughters moved into a house. The house was new to them, but it was, in fact, very, very old. Neighbors warned the family that the house was haunted. 'A girl was murdered. They never found the culprit.'" Willa told them about the creeper who'd been living inside a secret space inside the daughters' closet. How the ghost of the girl he'd murdered warned the daughters to hide under the bed before the man crept out one night and threatened the family with a knife.

When Willa finished, she scanned the group, hoping to catch a glimpse from one of them that said *I'm about to poop my pants*. But her friends looked skeptical.

"I don't get it," said Gray. "How did the family not know there was a *man* living in their house with them?"

"Happens all the time," said Willa, feeling defensive. "I read about it in the news."

"They put a ghost story *on the news?*" Sally asked.

Willa nodded defiantly. "I mean, I changed it around a tiny little bit. But yeah ... the *news!*"

"Ghosts aren't real," said Gray. "We only tell these stories to scare each other at slumber parties. None of them are actually true."

"Mine's true," said Martha, sitting up. She reached for the cap. Holding up the final scrap of paper, she showed everyone her name. Then she told them *her* story, the one that was true.

In August my family moved from a small town on the other side of the state. Way smaller than here and pretty far out from everything around it. Our house was surrounded by a preserve called the Great Swamp. Miles of wetlands. Dirt roads. People would drive in for hikes on wooden plank trails through the woods. From raised viewing huts, we'd watch birds and snakes and frogs and deer. And sometimes the snakes would eat the birds and frogs. And sometimes the deer would stare back at us like it was a contest of who would look away first. In the visitors' center, students from the college studied the habitat, and sometimes, my own sixth-grade class spent afternoons there, peeking at microscopic specimens in the lab.

The swamp was always very quiet.

Sometimes, it felt too quiet.

On one of the trails, there was the ruined shell of an old car from maybe like thirty or forty years ago. Someone had crashed it into a tree. It was all rusted out. Springs popped up from the seats. I always wondered how someone had driven it so far off the main road. Maybe the roads went a different way back then.

My classmates used to tell stories about the swamp. There was a legend that on certain nights, you could see green and blue lights glowing far off in the woods, gliding over the wetlands. They said that the lights were the ghosts of little kids who'd gotten lost in the swamp and had been dragged down by quicksand or snapping turtles. Some of my friends' older siblings swore up, down, left, and right that the lights were real. When I asked my parents about it, they said they'd seen them too, but that I shouldn't be scared.

According to them, the lights were natural phosphorescent gases coming up from the ground. Science!

Our house was about a half a mile from my bus stop at the visitors' center. In the fall, after school, I liked to listen to the last of the peeping frogs and chirping crickets there. I'd bring a comic book, and I'd read on a bench near one of the ponds until my parents returned from work, when they'd pick me up and drive me the rest of the way home.

One afternoon, I was still sitting on that bench when the sun slipped behind the trees. I had to walk. When I was only halfway down the road, it had grown almost totally dark. The sky was indigo, and the stars were appearing more quickly than I could count. I made sure to stay along the shoulder. Cars rarely passed that way at that time, but I thought it was better to be safe than sorry.

There was a crunching in the woods.

I turned to see a pale green glow, far off between the trees. Was it a ghost? A kid who'd gotten lost in the swamp? Or was it phosphorescent gas like my parents had said? I watched the green glow for several seconds until it flickered and blinked out.

I promised myself my parents were right. The crickets and tree frogs were blaring a reminder to keep going.

A few minutes later, I heard the crunching sound again—footsteps through dead leaves. This time it came from behind. I turned to see the green glow flickering a dozen feet back. I was about to run, but then I stopped and really looked.

The glow was strange and sort of beautiful. Didn't look like the swamp gas I'd imagined from my friends' stories or my parents' explanations. It was like . . . sunlight . . . caught inside a glass prism . . . hanging in a window.

What creeped me out was that it was so close.

"You're nothing but swamp gas," I whispered to it. It seemed to fade, and I tried to believe what I'd said.

I turned and continued on my way, noticing the glow from our front porch way off in the distance. I was worrying about where my parents were, and if they were all right, when those crunching footstep sounds came again, this time ahead of me. The glow emerged from the woods.

I bolted into the road.

The light seemed to shift, as if it were alive and watching. As if waiting for the right moment to come after me.

"You're nothing but s-swamp g-gas," I stammered. I ran toward our house, fast, the sound of crunching footsteps at my heels. The crickets and frogs called out, and in my mind, I imagined they were warning me to go, go, go, go, just like how I would do for the frogs and birds who were near snapping jaws out in the swamp. I shouted over my shoulder, "You're nothing but swamp gas!"

My driveway was just ahead. The porch light beamed across the front yard. I was at the door in seconds. I turned the key so hard, I nearly bent it. I slammed the door shut. "Nothing but swamp gas," I whispered again, this time, not believing a word of it.

Within minutes, I'd managed to turn on all the lights on the first floor, so I flopped onto the couch. The television blasted the evening news. When my parents pulled into the driveway, I had to stop myself from running outside and begging them to drive us far away, out of the swamp. They apologized for being late and asked if I'd made it home all right. I almost told them what had happened. But I didn't want to hear the one thing I knew they'd say: "It was nothing but swamp gas."

They'd brought Chinese takeout. We ate.

Upstairs, I was on the verge of sleep when I heard a noise in my room. A crunching sound, like the footfalls along the side of the road on the walk home.

I opened my eyes.

Beside my bed, I saw the figure made of light. Angular, overlapping shades of green, flecks of blue. Maybe there was a face inside. Maybe there wasn't. My jaw was locked shut. I couldn't scream or cry out. I couldn't move. And worst of all, I couldn't say what I needed to say: "You're nothing but swamp gas!"

The glowing figure seemed to lean toward me. When it spoke, its voice was like wind through hanging tree moss. It said: Sticks and stones may break my bones, but names will never hurt me.

Then, the thing was gone, and I could sit up again.

I called for my parents.

I told them I'd had a nightmare.

Nothing but a nightmare.

They left me alone. And I shivered under my covers till dawn.

Martha sat back on her heels and slumped her shoulders. The girls in the circle waited, wide-eyed, for more.

"Did you ever find out what it was?" Gray asked.

Martha shook her head. "Not swamp gas?" she suggested with a grin.

"And you never saw it again," Sally stated.

Martha shrugged mysteriously. "Not on that road. Not in that swamp."

A quiet fell on the girls. Then the dehumidifier clicked on in the mechanical room, and everyone jumped.

Willa clapped, startling her friends even further. "That was great!" she said. "Who wants more cookies?" It was obvious they'd all loved Martha's story best. Willa pushed aside a feeling of jealousy and reminded herself that it wasn't a contest. The stories were just a way to celebrate the season.

After they turned the lights off and finally got their giggles out, everyone fell into silence except Willa, who couldn't sleep. She looked at the clock on the window ledge. Digital numbers glowed red in the dark. Three o'clock. Someone had once told her that this was the Witching Hour, and it was bad luck for anyone to still be awake.

A few minutes later, Willa heard a strange sound. It made her think of someone walking through fallen leaves.

A greenish glow filled the room, reflecting off the wood-paneled walls. It looked just as Martha had described it. Almost like the shadow of a human, but made of light instead of dark. Willa pulled her sleeping bag up to her chin.

The thing hovered over the spot where Martha was sleeping.

Then, it focused on Willa, as if daring her to utter Martha's mantra . . . *Nothing but swamp gas.*

Willa kept her mouth shut. The overlapping angles that shifted inside the shape looked like a head tilting, considering her. It approached the basement wall, where Willa had taped the paper leaves. Its light reached out and touched them. The leaves began to glow, their edges rimed with shimmer, their colors growing brighter, like fireflies or will-o'-the-wisps or . . . like phosphorescent gas released from hidden pockets deep in the earth.

Willa's skin felt electrified. Instinct told her she should be afraid, but another sensation inside her grew stronger: a feeling of awe. Awe of this mysterious thing that was right in front of her. This curious presence that didn't seem intent on hurting her at all.

She sat up and watched the paper leaves glow.

She wanted to say *Thank you*. But before she could, the light was gone.

The basement was pitched once more into a blinding dark.

In the morning, when her friends awoke and begged for breakfast, Willa decided to keep the story to herself. Like her love for October, there were some mysteries too personal and impossible to explain.

THE NEW HOUSE

A mother, a father, and two daughters moved into a house. The house was new to them, but it was, in fact, very, very old.

Neighbors warned the family that the house was haunted. "A girl was murdered. They never found the culprit."

But the father scoffed. "There's no such thing as ghosts."

The daughters were to share the upstairs bedroom of the new house, the one with the wide windows and the big closet. Their parents would sleep in the one that was downstairs . . .

On the third night, the older sister woke to find someone shaking her arm.

A strange girl was staring down at her. The girl had dark hair, and her eyes were wide and fearful. She was dressed in a white dress, and her skin reflected the bluish moonlight that slanted through the windows.

The older sister flinched away from the girl's cold touch, but the girl held a trembling finger to her lips and then motioned quickly toward the dark gap under the bed . . .

Without thinking, the older sister grabbed at the little sister. Blinking away sleep, the sisters followed the girl silently down into the slim space.

"Who are you?" the little sister asked the girl. "Why are we hiding?"

The strange girl waved for the sister to be quiet. Seconds later, the closet door swung open with a soft squeal . . .

The sisters clenched their bodies and held their breath. Heavy footsteps knocked against the wooden floorboards. Closer and closer they came, until finally a pair of black leather boots stopped beside their hiding spot. The leather stank of damp and sweat and gasoline.

The older sister nearly yelped. Raspy breath came from

overhead. At any moment, the intruder would reach out and grab them . . .

But the person in the boots moved out to the hallway and down the stairs.

The little sister's words echoed in the older sister's mind: *Why are we hiding?*

"What about Mommy and Daddy?" asked the little sister.

From below, there came a blood-clotting scream . . .

The sisters ran to find their parents cowering in the kitchen.

A big man they didn't recognize was standing next to the table where the family had eaten dinner. The man was tall and broad-chested. There was a deep crease in his wrinkled forehead. On his feet were those black leather boots the sisters had seen while hiding under the bed. He wore a stained white T-shirt, dark pants, and a wide, tooth-filled smile . . .

"Who are you?" shouted the father, clenching his fists.

"What do you want?" yelled the mother, pulling a knife from the dish rack.

"Get out of here!" screamed the little sister.

The older sister clutched the younger's hand. "This is *our* house," she said, her voice a shard of glass . . .

Without a word, the man slipped out the back door and disappeared into the night.

The police came, and the sisters told them everything they'd seen.

Only then did they realize that the strange girl was gone . . .

The police investigated the bedroom upstairs. In the rear wall of the closet, they discovered a secret door behind which was a hidden room. Inside the room, they found a dirty sleeping bag, a musty pillow, a pair of threadbare socks, a flashlight, and food scraps stolen from the kitchen downstairs. On the walls, someone had scrawled strange sigils in thick black pencil. At the center of the sigils, a single word had been written. The word was *DECEMBER*.

The family sat together in the living room in horrified silence.

A man had been living in their closet . . .

Sometime later, another officer knocked at the door. They'd located the man hiding behind a garage across the street. They mentioned quietly to the parents that when they'd approached, the man's smile was still stretched across his face. The police had taken him away, sirens blaring.

Some people said afterward that he had been squatting in the house since before the family had bought it . . . Others had a different idea of where the man had come from—echoes of a local legend.

Some nights, weeks later, the older sister would lie awake, her little sister's question echoing through her mind, the fear in her voice as present as ever. *Why are we hiding?*

A few times, she had to tell herself that the man was gone. There was no need to crawl under the bed again. Instead, she would prop her desk chair beneath the knob of the closet door . . .

The sisters saw the girl once more. They'd visited the library to learn about their home and had discovered her picture in an old newspaper. The girl's address in the old paper was the same as the family's new house.

Her name had been Laura.

Laura Turner.

According to the article, witnesses had last seen Laura several blocks from home, talking with an odd man they described as tall and broad-chested, who was wearing black leather boots, a stained white T-shirt, dark pants, and a wide, tooth-filled smile . . .

A short time later, the man disappeared from the jail.

The sisters heard a rumor that authorities had found those same strange sigils scratched into the cinder blocks beside his cot. The word *DECEMBER* was there too. (Or was it a name? His name?)

Kids at their new school said the man had simply walked through the wall.

The older sister heard her sister's question in her mind once more: *Why are we hiding?*

Finally, she had an answer.

BABY WITCH

Everyone knows that there are witches out in the woods. Most of them live in a big old house that isn't like any house you've seen before. I won't describe it because you wouldn't believe me if I did.

The witches tend to look like you and me. But they're not. Some appear as girls and some as boys and some as neither and some as both. You might have already met one or two of them in town. Maybe more. The police officer? The teacher? The woman who runs the bookstore? The man who delivers the mail? You never can tell. Spend time peering into mirror glass, and you may find one of the witches peering back. It's possible they've stolen your face. Or maybe—just maybe— *you* are the witch.

Don't make them mad. If there is one deed that witches love, it's revenge. Ask anyone. They'll tell you it's true. But if you want to know *for sure* for sure, ask Bethany. She encountered one of them only last year.

It was out at Melissa Holcomb's house on Upper Yarrow Road.

The forest there used to be thicker. Impenetrable, they said. That was before the town decided that a business could cut them down and build the housing development where the Holcombs lived. You can be sure that this made those witches burn with anger.

Before she got to Melissa's, the girls from the dance crew sent Bethany a rhyme to memorize about the *Baby Witch*, who they said was the youngest of the coven in the woods. At the time, Bethany didn't believe in witches. She thought the silly rhyme was only part of an initiation.

Bethany was new to town. Everyone knows that after-school activities are a great way to make friends, so she'd tried out for the dance crew on a whim, even though she was aware she wasn't a very good dancer. What Bethany hadn't known was that the adviser, Ms. Ides, accepted all who wished to join. She also hadn't known that there was an unspoken rule among the eighth-graders that no one was to sign up unless Melissa Holcomb gave them permission first. Ms. Ides had once told Melissa, the crew captain, that her ideas were indispensable. How could a statement like that *not* have gone to poor Melissa's head?

On the day Bethany encountered the witch, the dance crew met in Melissa's living room. There were ten girls total, including Bethany. They sang:

Beware, beware the Baby Witch.

She goes out hunting with her switch.

When she swings, duck her lashes.

If she strikes, you'll turn to ashes.

Run away? You'll only maybe,

Dodge the witch who's still a baby.

Bethany repeated the rhyme in her head over and over, like a chant, as Melissa showed the group the new moves.

Beware, beware . . .

"Hands at your sides. Step forward with the left foot. Slide the right up to meet it."

. . . the Baby Witch.

"Cradle your arms, then UP! Clap over your head."

She goes out hunting . . .

"Lunge left. One knee bent. Keep your head facing left. Extend the left hand out. Hold the right at your shoulder, pointing your elbow in the opposite direction."

. . . with her switch.

"Lunge right. Other knee bent. Turn your head. Swing your right arm out and over. Bring your left hand to your left shoulder."

When she swings . . .

"Stand straight. Now snake your spine."

. . . duck her lashes.

"Bend at the waist. Face up. Reach both arms forward.

Good, now make your fingers all gnarly. Clutching."

If she strikes . . .

"Tuck down into a ball. Head between your knees."

. . . you'll turn to ashes.

"Look up. Smile wide . . . No. Wider!"

Run away?

"Hands on the floor. Kick both feet back behind you."

. . . You'll only maybe,

"Bend your elbows, chest to the floor, then roll to the right and hold, on your back."

Dodge the witch . . .

"Leap to your feet."

. . . who's still a baby.

"Peer over your left shoulder and bring your right fore-finger to your lips. *Shhhhhh.*"

Bethany was totally confused. While the other girls got the moves immediately, she stood off to the side and watched.

"See?" Melissa said to her friends with a clap and a smile. "Not so hard!" Then she glared at Bethany. "Let's try it again. *Everyone* this time."

"Why are we doing this?" Bethany asked. She hadn't meant to sound rude. But when the girls looked at her like her skin had turned green, she knew it had been a mistake.

"Why?" Melissa repeated.

Bethany knew she didn't have much experience when it came to dance crews, but this was unlike any cheer she'd heard before. Still, she made her voice sound sweet and full of curiosity. "Like, where are we performing it?"

"*Like*, right here?" Melissa answered. "There's something we do in dance crew called *practice*."

As if on cue, the girls all laughed. It struck Bethany as odd that they had the *same* laugh and they laughed for the *same* amount of time and their laughter was all at the *same* volume. As if they had practiced that too. As if it was part of the routine. "Oh. Right," she said. Her cheeks were on fire. She folded her arms across her chest, quickly recited the rhyme again in her head, then stepped in line with the others.

The group ran through the dance a few times. During the third round, Bethany finally felt like she could at least remember the moves, even if she had trouble executing them. After that, the girls went to the kitchen for a break. Mrs. Holcomb had left out a pitcher of cold water.

"You know she's real, right?" said Kristen, her lungs heaving.

"Who is?" Bethany asked.

"Baby Witch," said Fergie.

Melissa nodded. "She lives out in the woods with her family." She pointed to the thick growth of trees behind the house. "The coven."

Bethany chuckled at the joke. But the others were like stone. Their stares gave Bethany goose bumps. "A baby witch . . . lives . . . behind your *house*?" She sipped at her water, the cold glass tingling her fingertips and lips. She followed Melissa's gaze out the sliding door. Though the afternoon sun was shining, it was like all of the shadows between the trees had grown suddenly darker.

Melissa shattered the spell with a smile. "Come on, girls!" She waved them toward the door. "Let's see if we can conjure up Baby Witch!" Fergie and Kristen cheered and whooped as the crew poured outside onto a wide wood deck. Bethany put her glass carefully down on the counter and followed.

The house cast a wide shadow across the backyard. The woods seemed closer than they'd been before.

Melissa had the girls all line up as if they were on a stage facing the forest. "Bethany, you stand in front," said Melissa. "That way, we can make sure you're getting it."

There was nothing Bethany wanted to do less than stand at the front of the crew with her back to them. But this was what she'd signed up for, and if this was what it took to make new friends (even if they weren't very nice friends) then this was what she must do.

"Right!" said Melissa with a clap. "Is everyone ready?" The girls chimed in. Bethany glanced into the forest, scanning the spaces between the trees as if the witches' house might appear in the distance.

"Five, six, seven, eight!"

Bethany chanted as she tried to remember the moves. "Beware, beware the Baby Witch." Clap! Up! Over the head.

"She goes out hunting with her switch." Move the arm. Touch the shoulder. "When she swings, duck her lashes." Snake the spine. "If she strikes, you'll turn to ashes." Head between the knees. "Run away? You'll only maybe . . ." Pause on your back.

"Dodge the witch . . ." As Bethany stood, she realized that she was alone. The final piece of the rhyme leaked from her lips. ". . . Who's still a baby." She didn't bother peering over her shoulder or holding up her finger in a shushing gesture like she was supposed to. She was too entranced by the faces of the girls who were now staring from the other side of the door.

She'd been so caught up in getting the routine right, she hadn't noticed they'd all slipped back inside. Melissa stood in the center, sneering gleefully. There was a sharp clicking sound as the door locked. Muffled laughter came through the glass as the group turned away.

Bethany stood still. *This must be a joke. People aren't really this cruel.*

She bolted for the door. The kitchen was empty now. The girls were gone. Hiding.

Bethany looked toward the woods.

Beware, beware . . .

She rapped on the glass. Then she pounded. The door rattled. No one came. Not even Mrs. Holcomb, who'd said she'd be upstairs if anyone needed anything. *Had they planned this?* Bethany wondered. *Do they hate me that much?*

Beware, beware . . .

Hot shame flushed her skin. Her eyes burned. She wanted to run off. But her book bag was still inside. Her mother was coming to pick her up, but that wasn't for another hour. Bethany breathed slowly as she crouched on the deck.

Beware, beware the Baby Witch.

She hugged her ribs. It was growing chilly.

What a stupid rhyme. A stupid dance. Maybe Bethany didn't want anything to do with them anyway. *Maybe this is for the best.* She couldn't imagine falling in line behind those other girls, making her voice sound like theirs. Her laugh too. Bethany loved her laugh. It was one of her favorite things about herself. Wide-mouthed and clumsy and swooping and silly.

Beware, beware . . .

She'd change it all, though, right now, if only one of them would let her inside. She'd do the dance and smile at Melissa and agree with the rest of the girls that this was a very funny trick.

Bethany went down the steps to the lawn. Sitting at the bottom, she wiped her eyes. Then she noticed someone standing near the edge of the woods—a girl about Bethany's age. She wore strange clothes: a raggedy brown dress, shiny silver stockings that went up over her knees, a cluster of brightly colored ribbons tied at her wrists, black boots that were caked with dried mud. Her dark hair was long and curly, fairly greasy, and it was tied up on top of her head with another ribbon—this one acid green. As Bethany squinted, she could see blue markings on her neck. Drawings maybe?

After a long moment, the girl raised her hand—a half wave.

Bethany stood and brushed herself off.

"Are you crying?" the girl asked. Her voice was low; *velvety* was the word for it. Bethany imagined the girl was probably a really good singer.

"No," Bethany lied.

"You don't live here," said the girl.

"I'm visiting a friend," Bethany lied again.

The girl smiled, just barely revealing gleaming white teeth. "Sure you are."

Bethany puffed up her chest. "Who are you? What are you doing in the Holcombs' yard?" She'd never seen this girl at school. Maybe she went to the private academy the next town over.

"You know who I am," the girl answered, showing even more of those teeth. "You called to me."

Beware, beware . . .

"Very funny," Bethany answered, tucking a loose piece of hair behind her ear. "So, you heard me singing on the deck."

"The whole forest heard you," the girl replied, taking a step closer. She said it in a way that didn't sound mean. "You're lucky the rest of my family didn't come running. They're not as nice as I am."

Bethany felt suddenly bold. She imagined that any of the

other girls inside would have run away by now. "*You're* the Baby Witch?"

The girl laughed. Wide-mouthed and clumsy and swooping and silly. "What a funny thing to call someone. I mean, *clearly* I'm no baby. Not anymore, anyway."

Bethany paid attention to how that wasn't *quite* an answer. She could play this game too. "Where's your switch?"

"You want me to go home and get it?" the girl asked, her eyes bright and mischievous.

"I guess not," said Bethany. "I don't feel like ducking your lashes."

That laugh came again, and Bethany felt herself start to chuckle. It was as if everything that had just happened with Melissa and the others was ancient history. "I like you. You're fun," said the girl. Bethany blushed. "What's your name?"

"I'm Bethany. What's yours?"

"Oh, that's a secret," the girl said with a grin. She came up the slope and sat cross-legged on the grass at the bottom of the steps. "You should know better than to ever tell anyone your name. Just like in the fairy tales."

"But I told you mine."

"Exactly!" said the girl. "Your second mistake."

"What was my first?"

"Calling to me." The girl plucked a piece of grass, then held it up as if to examine it. "What were you crying about?"

"But I wasn't—"

The girl interrupted with a *tsk*. "They were mean to you? Those girls you were dancing with?"

Bethany pursed her lips. This was one of the strangest conversations she'd ever had. "They locked me out of the house. I'm sure they're just teasing."

"Sure. *Teasing*." The girl grabbed at Bethany's wrist. Bethany flinched, but the girl held tight. "Do you want my help? I'm very good at helping."

The pressure at Bethany's wrist felt warm, almost comforting. "Helping *how*?"

The girl's face lit. She sat up straight. Proud. "My family and I do all sorts of things for the people in this town. My father offers rides in his great big Pontiac to people who need them. My mother gave a deck of cards to one of our neighbors so her house guests could have some fun. We've thrown terribly exciting birthday parties for perfect strangers."

"Wow, that's nice of you."

"I'm really good at making figurines with the white mud you can dig up from under the Eden stones."

Eden stones? Bethany wondered.

"Sometimes, I leave the sculptures around, in people's yards, just to see little kids smile. And my siblings put together a book—a very special book—where if you read the stories, they come to life."

Bethany tried to pull her hand away again, but the girl only tightened her grip. "That's weird."

"It's not that weird when you belong to a family of witches."

"Hilarious," said Bethany, finally yanking her arm free. The girl's gaze went dark—darker than it already had been.

"Everyone knows that there are witches out in the woods," the girl went on. "Most of them live in a big old house that isn't like any house you've seen before. I won't describe it because you wouldn't believe me if I did."

Bethany felt a pressure in her lungs. This wasn't like a game anymore.

The girl kept talking. "The witches tend to look like you and me. But they're not. Some appear as girls and some as boys and some as neither and some as both. You might have already met one or two of them in town. Maybe more. The police officer? The teacher? The woman who runs the bookstore? The man who delivers the mail? You never can tell. Spend time peering into mirror glass, and you may find one of the witches peering back. It's possible they've stolen your face. Or maybe—just maybe—*you* are the witch."

Bethany was about to ask what that meant when the girl held up her hand.

"Don't make them mad. If there is one deed that witches love, it's revenge." The girl closed her eyes for a moment and shook her head, as if remembering. "Ooh, my family has a temper. You'd be shocked if I told you what my one auntie keeps in her basement. My granny can be real nasty if you keep her waiting when she's thirsty. If you hear her bell, you'd better come quickly. And my other auntie? She made sure to get back at those girls who scared her nearly to death. They have quite a talent for making people disappear."

"Your family turns them to ashes?" Bethany meant it to be a joke, to lighten the mood, as if that were possible, but she immediately realized her mistake.

The girl's glare was like icicles shooting into Bethany's brain. Then, all of a sudden, she let out a soft snort, and went on as if Bethany hadn't said a word. "Even *I* can go a little overboard some times. Once, I gifted my prized pumpkins to a family just down the road so they could make jack-o'-lanterns on Halloween. We all adore Halloween. But then the parents put those pumpkins out in their yard for the squirrels to nibble. No jack-o'-lanterns. No Halloween. No more family . . ." The woods were suddenly still; the birds and the peepers and the crickets hushed as if they knew something that Bethany didn't. "It was a real shame."

"Sounds like it," she answered quietly.

"Not many of the people who we've helped appreciate what we've done. Not like in the old days. Will you promise to appreciate me if I help *you*?"

This girl was certainly strange. What she'd just told Bethany about her family left her nerves tingling. But there was something about the way the girl looked at her—something hopeful, something excited—that caused Bethany to consider making a promise. "Help me *how?*" Bethany asked, her voice barely a whisper.

"You want to get inside that house, don't you?" The girl gestured up the stairs to the sliding glass door.

Bethany thought of her bag. Her homework and wallet and house keys. She nodded.

"You will *appreciate* my help?"

Bethany thought about that and then nodded again.

"And you'll *show* your appreciation? You'll tell your friends that I helped you? *You'll share your story?*"

Bethany felt her spine go stiff. She thought of the sneers on Melissa's and Kristen's and Fergie's faces. She thought of them laughing at her through the glass and then disappearing to another room. "Yes, I'll tell them. I promise."

The girl stood. "Good," she said with a smile. "I like helping new friends."

"*Friends?*" Bethany echoed. *This* was not the type of friend she'd imagined making when she'd signed up to dance.

"Sure, silly. I already told you that I like you." The girl held out her left hand, her palm facing upward. There was a bull's-eye in its center, drawn in blue ballpoint pen. With her other hand, the girl pulled a long black feather from inside her mouth. Bethany cringed. Even if it was just a magic trick, the feather must have been filthy.

But was it *just* a magic trick?

"Did you know some people believe that groups of crows

are angels?" The girl pressed the tip of the feather into her palm. "Like *actual* angels?" To Bethany's amazement, it stood erect, like one of the tall pines out in the woods. "They watch over us all, witches and humans alike. Crow angels don't discriminate, even if people barely ever listen to their advice."

"I didn't know that," Bethany answered softly. The black feather continued to stand in the girl's palm. Bethany was growing more confident that this was no trick. And she started to regret making a promise.

"Listen harder next time you hear them chattering away outside your bedroom window. You'll be surprised at their wisdom." The girl focused on the feather. "Quiet now."

In the moment before it happened, the world seemed at once both brighter and darker than it should have been. Nervous to make a peep, Bethany held her breath. Everything slowed. A cracking noise sounded from high overhead, or maybe it was well below the surface of the earth. Bethany glanced around, and when she looked back, the feather was ablaze. Bright light curled the feather's barbs. Its center stalk glowed orange, planted in the girl's palm as if by deep roots.

"How are you doing this?" Bethany asked.

Beware, beware . . .

She wanted to run, but she was frightened.

The girl glared at the house. "Look," she said.

Bethany found it difficult to rip her eyes from the burning feather, but when she did, she noticed something strange. All the windows in the house had gone gray. Soon, they turned black. "What did you do?" she asked. Intrigued, she climbed the steps. On the deck, she realized that the shadows at the windows were moving. Swirling smoke.

The girl was suddenly standing beside her, dark twists rising from the feather. "I'm helping." The girl smiled. "You wanted to get into the house, didn't you?"

Bam!

Something hit the door. Bethany screamed.

Bam! Bam! Bam!

Handprints appeared on the glass. The dance crew was in there. They couldn't get out. Something dropped to the floor against the glass just inside. A body?

Muffled screams broke out, followed by fits of wretched coughing. Bethany yanked on the handle, but the door wouldn't budge. She spun on the girl, who watched with an amused smile. "Stop it! You're killing them!"

"I'm *helping*."

Bethany's mind whirled. This was *not* what she'd meant. She would never have agreed—

A planter made of cement sat next to the door. Orange and yellow chrysanthemum blooms spilled over the edges. Bethany scurried to lift it, bending her knees, groaning as she stood, then tossed the planter at the door. A crashing sound broke the quiet. Shattered glass clattered to the ground.

Bethany closed her mouth and her eyes, expecting the

smoke to rush out at her, to smother her in a deadly hug. She waited. And waited. But after a few seconds, when nothing came, she opened her eyes again.

There was no smoke. Not inside the house. Not outside.

In fact, the only thing out of the ordinary was the shattered glass door and the crushed flowers and soil scattered across the kitchen's tile floor.

A voice called out, "What was that?" Melissa poked her head out from around a corner down the hallway. When she saw Bethany standing on the deck, the mess at her feet, she shrieked. She raced into the kitchen, the other girls following. "What is *wrong* with you?"

"But . . . but . . . ," was all Bethany could muster.

How could she explain that she'd been trying to *save* everyone? That she'd seen the house filled with smoke?

"Mom!" Melissa shouted.

Kristen came forward. "You've really done it."

Fergie's mouth twisted into a fearful grimace. "Are you *nuts*?"

Bethany turned to the girl from the woods, but she wasn't there. The backyard was empty. A quick breeze whipped across the grass. She heard a voice in her memory.

You'll show your appreciation? You'll tell your friends that I helped you? You'll share your story?

"Excuse me," Bethany squeaked, stepping over the broken glass. The other girls moved out of her way, as if she were dangerous. Someone to beware of. A bad girl. A witch.

Her bag was on the couch in the living room, right where she'd left it. She ran to the foyer just as Mrs. Holcomb was coming down the stairs.

"What's all the commotion?"

Bethany swung open the front door and hopped down all three steps to the brick path that led to the sidewalk. She ran in the direction of home, not looking back, not even when the girls called her name.

Her mother was waiting on the front porch. From the horrified look on her face, Bethany knew that Mrs. Holcomb had already been in touch.

Later, after her father had come from his office, after a torturous family dinner, after a long conversation about what was and was not an appropriate response to being bullied, Bethany made her way to her bedroom.

By then, the sun had gone down. The glow from her lamp had turned the window into a mirror. Bethany sat on her bed and stared at her reflection.

The witches tend to look like you and me. But they're not. Spend time peering into mirror glass, and you may find one of the witches peering back. Don't make them mad. If there is one deed that witches love, it's revenge.

The eyes of Bethany's reflection glinted strangely. Feeling a chill, she rushed to the window and drew shut the curtains. Outside, a crow cawed. She thought of the house out in the woods, the one the Baby Witch had said didn't look like any kind of house she'd seen before. She hoped *never* to see it.

There was something Bethany needed to do. She sat at her desk and took out some paper and a blue ballpoint pen. She began to write: *Everyone knows that there are witches out in the woods.* And she kept writing until she finally felt that the story was done.

Now, all she had to do was share it.

Just like she'd promised.

AMELIA IS INTERRUPTED

This time, it wasn't a bell that brought Amelia's attention away from the book, but a whistle.

Loud.

Piercing.

Endless.

At least until it ended.

Immediately, Amelia thought of her little brother. She imagined his expression when she'd left the house to come to the library alone. She thought of the girls in the story she'd just read, how mean they'd been to Bethany. Was leaving Win back at Grandmother's house the same kind of cruelty? If someone were to read her own story to her right now, would *she* be the bully? The villain? The Judge? The witch?

The sun had dipped farther in the sky, below the horizon now, so that the streaks of light no longer stretched across the wood floor. Instead, the light was ambient, glistening, warm— the kind of light Willa, the storyteller, must be fond of.

Amelia knew she should probably be getting back to Grandmother's house. But the book . . . the stories . . . She wanted to know *more.* She thought of Baby Witch—how there seemed to be a clue hidden inside that last tale which tied the others together in a knot. No, a net. She thought of how the Baby Witch had mentioned her siblings *putting together a book—a very special book—where if you read the stories, they come to life.* She remembered the bell she heard earlier and how Baby Witch had said her granny would ring for a glass of water. She thought of Auntie LaRue's chimney, where the man with the upside-down head hid during daylight hours, and the fireplace that gawped at her from across this very room?

Were *these* stories coming to life? Or was Amelia merely allowing the idea of them to grow in her mind, the spookiness of the stories clouding her thoughts and her senses? And what did this have to do with Grandmother, if anything?

In that last tale, the Baby Witch had said her family had "a talent for making people disappear."

Amelia shuddered at the thought of her grandparents being "turned to ashes" by a bunch of vengeful witches.

How likely was that?

Not very, she was almost certain.

Then, she remembered: Their last name had shown up in *another* story. The one about the man in the closet. About the ghost girl. Laura Turner. Amelia shivered. These names *meant* something. She was confident they did. But . . . she couldn't pinpoint exactly what.

Was there really a connection between her family and these tales? Between her dream of Grandmother and the place where she'd disappeared to?

DO NOT READ THIS BOOK.

There must *be more here,* she thought. Some real answers. *Logical* answers. And if she uncovered them, maybe she'd feel as satisfied as when she'd put together her class's yearbook, as when she gathered items for Grandmother's scrapbook. Objects that contained echoes. Tales. Just like the ones she'd been reading.

Amelia spread the pages wider, straining the book's spine, but then the whistle came again.

Loud.

Piercing.

Endless.

She jiggled her ear. The sound didn't stop.

Until it did.

She got up from the leather chair again, this time placing the open book facedown on the seat. Before she reached the doorway, a figure appeared. Images flashed through Amelia's mind: a raggedy dark dress, shiny silver stockings, ribbons tied at the wrist, black boots, blue markings on the neck.

Amelia held back a yelp. *Baby Witch?*

But it was only the librarian.

Mrs. Brown wasn't alone. She held the hand of a boy who was dressed in dizzying stripes—pants, shirt, and sneakers. Simply looking at Win made Amelia's head hurt, the same as when he whistled through the gap in his front teeth.

"I believe this belongs to you," said Mrs. Brown.

"Hi, Amelia!" Win chirped, like whenever he'd enter her bedroom uninvited.

"I found him in the children's section," the librarian went on. "I told him that if he wished to stay, he must be quieter."

Win held his finger to his lips. "Shhhh," he said, just like Melissa's choreography in the *Baby Witch* story. Because of his missing teeth, it came out *thhhh*.

"Win . . ." Amelia tried to control the quaver in her voice. "What are you doing here?"

"Grandmother's house was boring. Mama told me to come find you."

"*Mama* let you walk by yourself?"

"No, dum-dum. She brought me in the car."

Mrs. Brown cleared her throat and let go of his hand. "I've got some other patrons to attend to." She looked at Amelia. "You'll keep an eye on him?"

Amelia felt her cheeks heat up. "I guess I have to."

Mrs. Brown winked, then retreated down the hall.

Win eyed the book on the leather chair. "What are you reading?"

Amelia forced out a harsh breath to let him know she was *not* happy he'd shown up. "A book of scary stories."

"I love scary stories!"

"You do not. They give you nightmares."

"Not since I turned seven," he answered.

"Because seven's *so* different from six."

"Read them to me!"

Amelia wanted to scream.

Just then, an idea poked her. Right between the eyes. Some of these stories were fingers-down-your-spine, dread-making tales that pulsed like spider egg sacs about to burst. If she *did* read them to him, surely he'd leave her alone and wander back to the children's section, or maybe even up to Grandmother's house. Then, Amelia could continue her work deciphering the web that connected the tales to her dream, to her fear.

"*Fine,*" Amelia answered, the word like a dare. She eased down into her chair.

Win beamed and then raced for the other one. Hugged by the soft leather, he curled his skinny legs to his chest, wrapping them with his skinny arms. "This is *awesome,*" he whispered to himself, as if he were getting away with something forbidden.

Amelia grinned and smoothed the pages. She'd be alone again in no time.

SCREAMERS

Kelly and Dawn loved scaring people.

They'd drive around in Kelly's rusted-out pickup truck. Whenever they saw someone walking a dog or jogging or biking, one of them would lean out the window and bellow at the top of their lungs. Like this: "AHHHHHH!"

Oh, how funny they found it when the person walking the dog dropped the leash and the pup took off running. Or when the jogger jumped off the sidewalk. Or when the biker swerved into the curb. Kelly and Dawn would speed away, giggling like mad.

Causing trouble was a hoot.

Their first taste of it had been in Mrs. Fallon's fifth-grade English class. The teacher had been a stickler for students sitting in alphabetical order. Since Kelly's and Dawn's last names were next to each other, it was easy to switch seats. Mrs. Fallon usually didn't notice until halfway through the period, when she'd yell for them to get back to where they belonged.

The class would erupt in laughter.

During middle school lunches, one of them would dare the other to fake a fall while carrying an overloaded tray of pasta and sauce or some kind of mystery meat drenched in gravy. They'd toss the food as far as possible, guaranteeing a splash that would force the custodian to spend the next class period cleaning it up. After a perfect stumble, the entire cafeteria would ring with applause. Eventually the faculty caught on. Detentions were inevitable, but mostly, it was worth it.

As the pair careened through high school, bouncing off months and years and sometimes walls, Kelly and Dawn grew close. Kelly would share the latest maddening story of her father's strictness, her mother's absence, the unbearable loneliness that accompanied nightfall in a house where only one television channel was allowed to play. Dawn would tell Kelly how she often felt invisible compared to her *genius* older brother, who was destined for an Ivy League, how no matter the tutoring or how hard she tried, she'd never measure up in her parents' eyes. Making other people laugh, and more importantly, making *themselves* laugh was a way to forget the less than thrilling aspects of their lives.

One afternoon near the start of their senior year, Kelly and Dawn went for a ride. It was a clear day, the air as crisp as a fresh-picked apple. They turned out of the high-school parking lot. "Left-Right-Left game?" Dawn suggested. Kelly smiled. The Left-Right-Left game was as simple as it was pointless. The way it worked was: You turned left onto one street, then you'd turn onto the next street on the right. Then you took the next left, and then right, and so on. Depending on where they started, it was an effective method for finding new people to scream at. A few minutes after they'd begun, the girls found themselves heading into the hills outside of town, where the roads twisted and turned, and houses came farther and farther apart.

Dawn put her feet up on the dashboard and sighed. "This is the middle of nowhere."

"We're in luck," Kelly nodded. Up the road, a woman was crouched near her mailbox, planting flowers in a garden plot. Kelly pumped the brake. Dawn rolled down the window. The pickup slowed to a crawl, and Kelly veered closer to the side of the road.

The woman looked up. She wore a pair of faded denim overalls and a straw sun hat. Her gray hair curled out from under the brim. She looked curious, as if she might find an old friend stopping in for a surprise visit. When she saw the girls, she scrunched her brow.

Dawn leaned out the passenger-side window. She opened her mouth and filled her lungs, and then released one of her most blood-churning screams ever.

The woman's expression turned to shock. Her eyes bugged out and her jaw dropped. A shudder rattled her, and she fell backward into the bed of bright orange chrysanthemums, crushing most of the blossoms.

Kelly watched from behind the wheel as the older woman's feet went up in the air. This was a new reaction—an *amazing* reaction, in her opinion—and she howled with laughter as she slammed her foot against the gas pedal and peeled off down the street.

Minutes later, after the girls had worked the giddiness out of their systems, wiping tears of laughter from their eyes, they drove in silence. Red-cheeked, Dawn turned to Kelly and said, "Do you think she's all right? Should we go back and check?"

"Aww, she's fine. Do you want to get caught?"

Dawn shook her head.

"Great, then help me find our next victim."

But Dawn said she was feeling carsick, and she wanted to go home.

Kelly was surprised; Dawn was always up for screaming.

"See you tomorrow, loser," Kelly called out as Dawn trekked up the driveway. Dawn didn't look back.

That night, Kelly was sitting at her desk in her bedroom when her phone rang. It was Dawn. She was sobbing. "What's up?" Kelly asked. She hated when people cried in front of her.

"Did you hear the news?"

Dawn had listened to it over her uncle's police scanner. The older woman, whose last name was November—the one who'd toppled into the chrysanthemum patch that afternoon—had been found by her husband lying underneath the mailbox. She'd had a heart attack. Mrs. November was dead.

Kelly yelled at Dawn to stop joking around. Stuff like that wasn't funny. But Dawn wasn't joking.

"We can't tell anyone what we did," Kelly whispered.

Dawn agreed.

Later, Kelly brushed her teeth and crawled under her covers, thinking about the poor woman laid out in the flowers as she and Dawn had zoomed away, about how hard she and Dawn had laughed as they'd left her alone, about how she must have died staring up at the leaves turning on the branches overhead.

In bed, in the dark, Kelly felt numb. Downstairs, the television blared. Her father was watching that horrible news show again. Worry fluttered through Kelly's mind.

This wasn't supposed to have happened. Screaming was meant to be fun. Funny. But also, it was a way to let out frustration and anger and fear. Kelly imagined once that the people she and Dawn frightened must have found it funny too—afterward, at least. Unfortunately for the woman today, there would be no afterward.

Hours later, once the house had gone quiet, Kelly slid into a delicate sleep. When the step at the bottom of the stairs let out a *creak*, her eyes opened like a trap.

It was probably just her dad grabbing a glass of milk from

the kitchen or running to the bathroom.

Another creak. Another step. Then another and another. Someone was climbing the stairs.

Kelly slumped against the mattress and yanked the blanket up to her nose. The streetlamp outside filtered in through gauzy curtains, casting a pale glow on the opposite wall. She stared at her bedroom door, thankful it was shut.

There was a *thump, thump, thump, thump* just outside, as if someone were walking on their heels. This wasn't her father. This was someone else. Kelly had an idea who, but she forced it from her mind. The dark sometimes pulled impossible things up from the depths. She glanced at the phone on her bedside table, wondering if she should reach out to Dawn. Hearing her best friend's voice might help.

A squeak came from across the room. The doorknob was turning. Slowly. Slowly. Kelly gulped breath, then wrenched the blanket up over her head. She couldn't stop herself from trembling as the door swung open.

Footsteps entered her room.

Please, no, thought Kelly. *I'm sorry. I'll never play the screaming game again. Just leave me—*

The footsteps stopped. Kelly exhaled. Slowly. Slowly. She listened through the covers.

Someone tapped Kelly's shoulder.

She jolted so hard, the blanket slipped halfway off the bed.

A figure was backlit by the bluish haze of the streetlight

through the window. Kelly stared at the figure, unable to move. The figure stared back. Even in the dark, Kelly made out a pair of denim overalls. The person's head was a halo of shadow, and Kelly remembered the old woman's straw hat.

Kelly tried to speak. *Get out!* Or *I'm sorry!* But her voice stuck in her throat.

The woman leaned forward, placing her hands flat on the mattress. The smell of chrysanthemums and soil wafted forth, and Kelly nearly choked as she pressed herself down against her pillow. The woman let out a shriek so loud and terrible, Kelly felt the bed go damp.

Her breath was sucked from her lungs and a pressure thumped her sternum. She tried to flail her arms out, but they were pinned to her sides. The only thing she could do was squirm like a worm on a fishing hook. She fell to the floor, landing partly on her blanket, her hip crashing into the hardwood with a crunch. (If this had been at school, her classmates would have shrieked with applause.) The blow was enough to shock her back into her body, and she kicked herself away from her bed until her spine was against the wall. Kelly raised her hands.

But the woman was gone.

Wiping her eyes, Kelly peeked under the bed. Clear. She hobbled to her feet, her hip aching, and then crept to the closet. Except for clothes on hangers and a messy pile of shoes, it was empty. The bedroom door was closed. Kelly opened it and checked the hallway. No one was there. Oxygen swept into her chest—cold and shocking. She was more awake now than ever.

Kelly grabbed her phone. She dialed Dawn's number and waited as the tone beeped on the other end of the line. There was a click and an inhalation, and before her friend could even say hello, Kelly spewed her story. She told the whole thing in a single breath, practically, and when she was done, she waited for Dawn to respond, to say that Kelly had been dreaming or that she was being paranoid. She almost hoped that Dawn accused her of lying so she could scream back and let out all of this horrible fear and frustration and make her friend feel as bad as she did.

But Dawn didn't answer.

Instead, another voice spoke. "I already know all of this, sweetheart." The old woman chuckled, not sounding amused—more like *satisfied*. "I was there."

Kelly glanced at the phone. Its light was dark. She tried to swallow. Tried to answer. But her throat felt like it was closing up.

"See you tomorrow night, dear," Mrs. November added. "And the night after that. And the night after that. And the night after—"

Kelly threw her phone at the floor, letting out a shriek to wake the dead.

THE PSYCHOPATH'S TAROT

I t is dusk when you arrive at the house in the woods.

"We made it!" says Tae from the passenger seat.

Kylie shifts the gear into park, rolling her eyes, exhausted from the two-hour drive.

The log cabin is surrounded by birch trees, white paper bark blending into the snowy landscape like camouflage. The roof is steeply pitched tin that makes heavy snow slide right off. Porch lights cast a golden glow onto untouched white. Several windows beam slatted illumination through drawn blinds.

"As pretty as always," you say.

It is the Friday after Thanksgiving, your senior year of high school. You've been friends with Kylie and Tae since kindergarten. Even though you three are totally different, and always have been, you think of them as your forever sisters, and you can't imagine what life will be like when you all go off to separate colleges next fall. The cabin belongs to Tae's family. Mr. and Mrs. Brewster will be here tomorrow.

They were kind (and trusting) enough to let you three come up early after you'd all practically begged for the chance. The weekend won't be all fun and games and food and snow, however. On Monday, you'll have to turn in your story about the girls' soccer team to the editor of the school paper. Thankfully, you've written half of it already.

From the back seat, you pat Kylie's shoulder. "We can relax now." Through the rearview mirror, she tosses you a smile.

Tae has to try the key several times before the lock turns. Once inside, you plop your duffel down onto the couch and look around. The ceiling soars. A small staircase leads up to a balcony room. "You take that one," Tae tells you. "Me and Kylie in the guest room, on the trundle beds. My parents' room is across the hall."

"I remember," you answer. The balcony has always been your favorite. You love the view in the mornings.

You put on a kettle of water and pour powdered chocolate into three mugs. The hot tub on the patio out back had been set at seventy, and it's going to take a few hours before it's ready.

Kylie blasts some unfamiliar music on the stereo. It's like fingernails on a chalkboard, but you say nothing. She bops around for a bit before examining the books on the shelves under the windows.

"What game should we play first?" you ask, holding your hand over the kettle spout, impatient for the water to boil. "How about Passwords?"

"That one's better with more than three people," says Tae. "Maybe Monopoly?"

"Too stressful," says Kylie. You laugh, remembering what happened the last time you three opened that box.

"Parcheesi is always a good time," you suggest.

"For our grandparents," Tae mutters.

"We could attempt the new one I brought," you say. "There are these cards that—"

Kylie interrupts. "What about *these* cards?" She pulls a deck from the bookshelf. On the front of the box is the image of a dark-haired man in white and red robes. One hand points at the sky. The other points to the ground. On a table before him sit a number of strange objects. A word pops into your head. *Magician.*

Tae gasps. "That's not a *game*. Those are tarot cards."

"Duh," says Kylie. "My auntie has this same deck."

You shake your head. "What are they for?"

"Telling the future." Kylie sits at the table in the small kitchen, opens the box, and removes the contents. She fans the cards out before her. The backs are dark blue and covered with tiny white stars.

"Where did they come from?" Tae goes on. "They don't belong to *my* family. Our pastor says—"

"Is your pastor here?" Kylie asks all honey-eyed, with a hint of spice. Tae clamps her mouth shut. "Anyone want a reading?"

There's a pause in the music. The kettle begins to whine. Before it can scream, you snatch it off the burner and fill the mugs. "I'll take one if you do one for yourself first."

Tae crosses her arms. "Pastor Jane says cards like those are—"

"Loads of fun," Kylie says. You place a mug before her. You hand another to Tae. "Now sit down. Both of you."

Minutes later, you've dimmed the lights and the music. A candle flickers inside a glass sleeve in the center of the table. Tae sits across from you, wearing a dubious expression, but she knows enough to not go up against Kylie when Kylie has her mind set. Kylie shuffles the deck end over end and then cuts it in two before fluttering the cards back into a single pile. She divides the pile in thirds and then puts it randomly together again. She does this twice more and then sets them facedown beside her steaming hot chocolate.

"Aren't you supposed to ask a question or something?" Tae mentions.

"Oh, but I have," Kylie answers with a grin. She holds a finger to her temple. "In here."

"What did you ask?" You think about everything *you'd* like to know. *Which school will you get into? Will Jillian Yi ask you to the prom? How can you stop graduation from putting a period at the end of your friendships?*

"It's a secret," says Kylie mysteriously, turning over the first card and setting it onto the table. She stares at the card with a look of bafflement.

"What's wrong?" asks Tae.

Kylie answers slowly. "I know this deck. But I've never seen this card before."

You and Tae lean in for a better look. The image on the card shows a silhouetted figure standing in some dark woods. Overhead, a starry sky tries to peek through spotty clouds. The person in the picture is clutching something sharp, held against their leg.

"That's creepy," says Tae. "What's it mean?"

Kylie shakes her head and picks up the box the cards came in. "It shouldn't be in here." After reading the brief description on the box, she picks up the deck and flips it over. Rifling through the images, she looks satisfied. "*These* are the cards I remember." Then, pointing at the weird one on the table, she says, "Maybe this one is just a fluke, shuffled in from a different deck."

"Toss it out?" Tae suggests.

"But I *picked* it." Kylie squints. "We can make up our own meaning."

Tae blinks, unsure.

"What's it mean to you?" you ask.

"Well, this position usually represents the question itself," Kylie answers. "My auntie says you can discern what a card says by looking at the cards surrounding it. Each card in the sequence is like a sentence in a story."

"So, then, what's the next sentence?" Tae asks.

Kylie picks another card and places it crosswise on top of the first card, then brings her hand away quickly, as if it might bite.

This one resembles the one underneath it, that same figure holding that same sharp object, clearly a knife. However, on this card, the dark figure is walking through the woods. The look on Kylie's face tells you everything. "*This* card isn't supposed to be in the deck either," you say.

Tae frowns. "Are you messing with us?"

Kylie shakes her head. "When I flipped through a second ago, this card wasn't here. You saw for yourself."

You think of the winding roads that brought you up into these hills. You think of the many acres of thick forest that separates you from the last town you passed. How many miles back was it?

"I don't like this," says Tae, pushing her chair away from the table.

Kylie is eager to pull the next card, to figure out what's going on. She lays it on the table in a spot between herself and the previous two cards. This one shows that the figure has entered a clearing. Starlight shines down from above. Now you can see the figure is dressed in a black sweatshirt, black jeans, black boots with thick soles. The face is weirder, pale and plastic-looking, with empty eye sockets. Rumpled dark hair sticks up from its head in haphazard chunks. Clearly the face is a rubber Halloween mask.

"How is this happening?" Kylie whispers.

"My pastor says playing with cards like these is evil," says Tae.

"It is *not*!" Kylie insists. "My auntie goes to church just like you do. This is . . . a message. An answer to my question."

"What was your question?" you ask.

Kyle glances down at the spread of cards. "I feel like now I shouldn't tell you," she whispers. "I don't think you'd want to know."

"You can't do that to us!" Tae exclaims.

Kylie shushes her and draws another card. You can see frustration burbling on Tae's face, and you're beginning to feel similarly. Kylie places her new card on the left side of the first two—another nighttime scene, but instead of a shadowy figure, there's a snow-covered hillside.

"Is *this* one a regular card?" you ask. "From the regular tarot deck?"

Kylie gives her head a quick shake. Drawing three more, she places one above the first two. The next, she puts to the right of the first two. All together, they form a *T*. The third she lays down separately, to the far right of the *T*.

You all lean closer to see the further pieces of this strange story. The card at the top of the *T* shows a spotlight at the hill's crest. The next card is the shadowy figure crawling through the snow on all fours, still clutching a long, glinting knife. The card on the far right makes your blood feel like ice—the house on it looks exactly like the cabin.

"Put them away," Tae says. She stands up, her feet skidding back from the table.

"But I want to see how the reading ends," Kylie says, a mystified look on her face. Curiosity can sometimes make people appear enchanted.

"Tae is right," you add. "This is wrong. Especially since you won't tell us what your question was."

Kylie ignores you both. She takes another card off the deck and puts it above the card on the far right. Here, you see the scattered birch trees surrounding the back patio, where clouds of steam rise from the heating tub.

That figure is crouched behind it.

"This isn't funny!" Tae claps her hands hard, and Kylie flinches.

"I'm not doing anything. I swear."

You get up and go to the window at the rear of the house and peer outside.

"What do you see?" asks Tae.

The spotlight illuminates the patio. The clouds have broken; starlight shines. Mist hovers over the hot tub. The light doesn't reach beyond. "Nothing," you answer unsurely.

There's a shout and a scuffle. You turn to find Kylie and Tae tussling over a card. Kylie had pulled another one, but Tae doesn't want her to place it on the table.

You push the girls apart. "Cut it out!" Kylie clutches the card, her chest heaving. "You're scaring us, Kylie."

"Maybe we *should* be scared," she says. "When I shuffled the cards, in my mind, I asked if we were going to have fun this weekend." We all take in what she is suggesting. "What if the cards *are* a warning?"

"That's impossible," says Tae. "There's no such thing as magic."

Kylie's face pales as she glances at the card in her hand. "Then how do you explain this?" She places it above the previous one. As soon as you see the image, you feel the few sips of hot chocolate winding their way back up your esophagus. The image is focused on the rear of the cabin, at the window overlooking the patio. Someone inside the house is holding the blinds open. Wide eyes stare out into the night.

It is an illustration of you—of where you were standing a moment earlier.

You don't know if this is magic or a miracle or maybe even a nightmare. But you've had enough. "That's it!" you yell, scooping the cards into a messy pile. "We're done."

"Hey!" Kylie shouts.

"I want to leave," Tae says.

Kylie's anger drops away. "What? No! I'm sorry! Let's do something else. I'll make dinner. Pasta and salad. Maybe there's something fun on television. Sound good?"

You stare at her, holding up the mess of cards. "How can you be okay with this?"

"Want me to go outside and look around? Will that make you feel better?"

"No!" you and Tae both shout. You all glance at each other for a few silent seconds.

Kylie's gruffness falls away. "Listen," she begins again. "I'm really sorry. Let's just . . . forget it, okay? You're right. There's no such thing as magic. I bet we'll figure out an explanation when your parents arrive tomorrow, and then we can laugh about it. Right?"

After a second, Tae lets out a slow sigh. "What kind of pasta sauce did you bring?"

Your skin is electric. Your friends don't get it. But then, *they* didn't see themselves on an actual card. You straighten out the deck, shove the cards into the box, and then stick it on the shelf. You press your lips shut, unsure if you should mention your fears.

Tae clicks the remote. Obnoxious voices of local news anchors resound. Kylie turns on all the lights and then gets to work in the kitchen. You decide to make sure the bathroom is super clean. It helps settle your mind. After dinner, you all sit down for a few episodes an old sitcom from when you were kids. You force your laughter to drown out any thought of the "reading."

Later, when Kylie suggests that you all put on your bathing suits and head out to the hot tub, you refuse to think about what that second-to-last card was hinting at. As you slip into the frothing tub, you take in the snow-covered hillside that leads toward the line of trees. This feels like an act of defiance. Gesturing rudely at Fate.

In the distance, there is the yipping and yelping of some sort of canine. "Coyote pups," says Tae with some confidence.

"You think their mama's nearby?" The pups continue to cry as your face turns red and the heat makes you sweat.

After you climb the steep stairs to the balcony, after you slip under the chilly covers, you push your conflicted thoughts down and wonder how you'll spend the day tomorrow. Tae's parents won't arrive until the afternoon. Maybe you'll drive into town for breakfast. And later, you'll try for a hike on the trails to one of the local caves. Maybe the waterfalls have frozen over. You'll bring your camera; maybe you'll capture something *truly* magical. Then you remember: Your essay is also waiting.

You wake with a start, wondering for a moment where you are. You sit up. The darkness feels like someone stealing your breath. You reach for the lamp next to the bed, and when the glow reaches across the balcony floor, you remember that you're at the cabin.

Downstairs, one of your friends is snoring softly. Tae probably. She's the heaviest sleeper.

Cold shocks your bare feet on the floor. You make your way downstairs to the bathroom. As you wipe sleep from your eyes, you feel a sudden panic. Through the blinds, you can see the spotlight illuminating the patio at the rear of the cabin. Someone forgot to turn it off.

Your vision lands on the bookshelves beneath the window. Curious, you kneel. Your fingers settle on the box. You take the cards into your lap.

There was one card left in Kylie's spread—one last sentence in the story the cards were trying to tell.

Curiosity *is* a type of enchantment. You're under its spell now. You find yourself sitting at the table in the small kitchen. The candle in the center flickers as you let the cards pour through your hands, again and again. You divide the deck in two and then flutter the cards back into a single pile. Then, just like you saw Kylie do earlier, you cut the deck in three and then put it together again. You do this twice more.

You know what's going to happen.

You want to stop. But something won't let you.

You place the deck facedown.

Shadows dance all around.

At the end of the hall, someone's breath halts, then settles back into a steady rhythm.

You reach for the card on top. You know what you will find there, but you turn it over anyway. A pale face is at the rear window, empty eye sockets peering through a gap in the blinds, the tip of the blade *tap-tap-tapping* against the glass.

It is, in fact, the last sentence in your story.

THE HAPPY BIRTHDAY MAN BIRTHDAY CAMP

While riding his bike on a humid late-summer afternoon, a few days after a disappointing twelfth birthday, James Fuller happened upon a street he'd never noticed before. He wasn't far from home, but finding the nameless road made him feel adventurous and brave.

While most of the streets by James's neighborhood veered around ravines and rocky outcroppings, this road was as straight as the path of a crow flying. Leafy branches reached out and formed a shadowed tunnel. James pedaled slowly. His bike bumped over hard-to-see pebbles, and he swerved around several deep potholes.

Ahead, a fleck of color appeared in the thick brush at the side of the road. Riding closer, James discovered a sign nailed crookedly to the thin trunk of a sapling. Red letters were scrawled on a white wooden plank. They read: THE HAPPY BIRTHDAY MAN BIRTHDAY CAMP. Painted below, an arrow pointed down the forlorn road in the direction he'd been heading.

Quiet rang in his ears.

Earlier that week, James had masked his disappointment that his parents would be working in the city during his birthday. Only his older brother and sister, Jared and Jessica, had been around to celebrate, and they were already busy with summer jobs. His siblings had bought a small, too-sweet cake at the Price Chopper, but they'd been barely able to muster up the energy to sing him the dang birthday song. His parents had left him a single gift to open by himself. There hadn't even been a card. Unwrapping it, he found an old copy of *Through the Looking-Glass*. Why would they think he'd want to re-read a story for actual babies? He'd tossed the book in a drawer and spent the rest of the night watching a documentary about dragon mythology.

Now he wondered if all of that had been a trick. Maybe his family had placed this sign in the trees as a clue to an *actual* birthday surprise? But how could they have known he'd come this way?

James let go of his bike. It clattered to the ground. "Hello?" he called out. No one answered. He stepped closer to the sign.

The Happy Birthday Man? He imagined costumed characters at fast-food restaurants and those animatronic animals that sing to you, unblinking, from dusty stages at run-down pizza-party parlors in those scary-as-heck video games meant to give kids like him heart palpitations.

"Jessica? Jared?"

Birds chirruped, high and far away.

The sign's paint looked fresh. He poked at it, and his finger came away tacky. Ignoring the prickly sensation in his chest, James continued in the direction of the jagged arrow. The path grew thin. The asphalt turned to gravel, then dirt, muddy in spots, the path sloping slightly and then rising up to meet bedrock before sloping slightly again.

A memory came to him of walking here some time ago. Had he dreamed of it? In that dream, had he heard a voice in his ear whispering, *Don't go down there*? Had it been the same voice that was whispering now?

Don't go down there . . . Right in his ear, as if someone's lips were inches away.

James flinched and flailed and then lashed out at the person beside him.

But no one was there.

His heart pounded, his forehead chilled with sweat.

James couldn't see the sky anymore. The shadows were darker now. The path dipped, as if worn by decades of travelers. Hikers. Horses. The brush was so dense, he couldn't have wandered off if he'd wanted to.

Ahead, the trail dropped off into nothingness. Coming closer, James discovered that a great chunk of the earth had given way. Roots dangled over the muddy edge. Below, trees rose up, carpeting the bottom of the gully. Across the ravine, he noticed a divot in the landscape, a dark hole in the canvas of the forest. He figured that the birthday camp, if there were such a place, would be just beyond.

Unreachable.

James was about to turn back when he heard a soft chiming.

Someone across the ravine was waving at him. James squinted. The person wore a strange costume, a one-piece suit that reminded him of pajamas, decorated with black and white horizontal stripes. The dingy fabric bunched at the cuffs and billowed slightly. A dark collar circled the person's neck, from which dozens of black strings hung, each tied with what looked like sleigh bells. Shadows blocked the person's face.

Were they warning him away? Or were they signaling for him to come closer?

"Are you all right?" James called.

The person shouted something that James couldn't make out. They waved their arms harder.

The bells went *jingle-jangle, jingle-jangle.*

"Stay there! I'm going for help!"

He ran up the dirt trail. When he reached his bike, he raced back along the path, steering around the potholes and pebbles.

Up the road.

Around the corner.

Toward home.

Bursting into the house, James cried out, "Jessica! Jared!"

When his sister drove him back, the road wasn't there anymore. Instead, there was a thick wall of brush. "Is this supposed to be a joke?" Jessica asked.

"Not funny," Jared said.

James stepped out of the car and stared into the forest. "It was *here*. I swear." He felt shakier now than when he'd reached the cliff's edge. "The road turned to a trail that stopped at a ravine. Someone was on the other side. They were dressed like . . . like a clown. They were waving like they needed help."

Jared raised an eyebrow. "So, this road just *disappeared*?"

James was suddenly unsure. The asphalt seemed to shift, and he caught himself on the hood of the car.

At home, his siblings gave him ginger ale and made him lie on the couch. His parents were still in the city. Jessica called them, then handed the phone to James.

"What happened, honey?" his mother asked.

"I got confused," he admitted. "I don't think I'd had enough water."

"Be more careful next time," said his father.

Next time . . .

When Jared offered James the last of the too-sweet birthday cake, he refused, so Jared ate it himself. Jessica turned on a silly cartoon show, perching on the edge of the recliner, glancing with concern at James for the rest of the evening.

That night, James dreamed of the road to the Birthday Camp. It was just as it had been, the dappled tunnel stretching before him. Ahead, someone was walking. James called out, but the person didn't turn around. He ran down the path, desperate to know who it was, only to catch up to the figure and find that the person was himself.

Himself from before.

From yesterday.

"Don't go down there," he said to the kid he was yesterday.

Yesterday James turned, flailing.

"I'm sorry!"

Yesterday James walked onward.

The trail started to close in on them. "Listen to me," James practically shouted. A ringing echoed through the woods. *Jingle-jangle, jingle-jangle.*

He sat up in bed.

But the noise didn't stop.

Where was it coming from? It grew louder. Was it in his head?

Jingle-jangle, jingle-jangle.

James turned on the lamp, stood, and listened. The sound was coming from his dresser. Creeping over carefully, he slid open his top drawer. Nestled on a pile of socks was a collar of bells, like the one James had seen the person in the woods wearing. Who had put it in his drawer? How had it been ringing?

He held up the collar. Long strings dropped down, swinging and chiming. He pulled them taut, and they cried out.

A breeze came through his open window, sending goose bumps across his skin. Someone had told him once that you can't feel goose bumps in your dreams.

He was curious to see what they felt like. He slipped the collar over his head. The bells came down past his waist.

Jingle-jangle . . .

Looking down, he saw that the floorboards of his bedroom were gone.

Now he was walking barefoot along a dirt path. Green brush surrounded him. The overcast sky was a threat. James realized that he was dressed in a striped union suit—black and white and dingy like the one the person across the ravine had been wearing yesterday, silver snap buttons gleaming from his stomach to his throat. *How did I get here?* he wondered. *Was it the collar of bells? Am I still dreaming?* James stumbled over thick brush and fallen branches. Sharp things poked at the soles of his feet. The bells rang as the strings smacked against his body.

Jingle-jangle . . .

Odd colors appeared in the corners of his vision. Bright shades that didn't belong in the woods. Or wherever this was. He left the path to find several boxes decorated with purple marbled wrapping paper and tied with acid-colored ribbons and bows that puffed out, bigger than his head.

There was a card attached to one. He plucked it like a piece of fruit. His name was written in elaborate swirling black cursive. Tearing open the envelope, James removed a piece of white card stock marked with red polka dots. A message read: *For James, No one should have to celebrate a birthday alone. With love, The Happy Birthday Man.*

James pulled off the ribbon and bow. He tore away the marbled paper to find a square brown box. Lifting the lid, James looked inside. White tissue paper was spotted with red, but these marks weren't polka dots. He lifted out the contents and then unraveled the tissue. When he saw what was hidden there, he threw it to the ground. In the middle of the paper there was gristle and bones and grease—the remains of someone's lunch.

A sick joke.

James looked to the other presents. He noticed that one of them appeared to be wet on the bottom, as if something inside was leaking. The wrapping paper was stained red. The box next to it looked all right, decorated just as beautifully as the first one. As he stared at it, something knocked from within. When the box rolled toward him, James backed away. The gift juddered across fallen leaves, heading for his bare toes.

James felt his hair rise. He took off into the woods. The path was no more. Every few steps, he thought he saw another gift half hidden behind a tree or buried in a pile of brush. He thought of the message: *No one should have to celebrate a birthday alone.* All he wanted right now was to wake up at home. He wanted his family. His brother and his sister. His dad. His mom, sitting on the edge of his bed, singing him to sleep, her voice like a beautiful bell that warned off bad dreams.

James almost didn't see the ground start to slant. He fell onto his side and then skidded to a stop, his legs dangling over a rough, rocky edge.

He was back at the ravine.

Blood beaded where he'd scraped his knee. If you can't feel goose bumps in dreams, he thought, you definitely shouldn't be able to feel pain. *Is this a dream or not?* he wanted to shout. But to whom? The Red King from the looking-glass in that Alice story?

The landscape before him was a reflection of what James had seen the previous day. Then he realized he was on the opposite side of the ravine now, where he had seen the person waving to him . . . The person who had been wearing a collar of bells. And a dingy black-and-white union suit.

The person who had looked exactly as James did right now.

Standing, James tore at the silver buttons, but they wouldn't give. Neither would the collar. He yanked the bells but the strings were strong. The bells rang raucously. He shouted and grunted as he struggled to rip through the costume.

Soon, he was panting and exhausted, but no closer to getting the collar, or the costume, off. Movement caught his eye. There was a boy across the ravine. James raised his hand and waved. The bells made a commotion, and the boy saw him. He called out something James couldn't understand. It was like the space that separated them had chewed up his voice. The boy was familiar. He wore a blue T-shirt and red shorts with white piping, just like what James had worn yesterday . . .

He was looking back at himself.

James called out, "It's dangerous! Keep away!" He remembered that the James he'd been yesterday hadn't understood him. He raised his arms and waved. But the jingling bells would only make the other James—the *before* James—more curious.

"Stay there!" yesterday James called back. "I'm going for help!" It sounded choppy, almost unintelligible, but James knew what the other boy had said, because he'd been the one who'd said it first.

A moment later, yesterday James was gone. The *now* James would have to find his own way across.

Quaking, he listened to the sounds of the forest—that high-pitched scream of bugs and birds and frogs. He had to keep going. He had to get home.

Maybe there was a path that led along the ravine's edge. Or he could try climbing down and then up the other side. Ahead, a neon-red object caught his attention. A large rosebush made entirely out of twisted balloons stood beside the trail. Along the clearing, more balloon flowers grew, forming a path of their own. He thought of the beautifully wrapped boxes. These were different, no? He could almost see himself in the reflection of the rubber. Before he could stop himself, he'd reached out and touched one of the flowers.

It popped. James stumbled away, his bells jangling again. His nerves too. He kept still, eyelids fluttering, trying to catch his breath.

A whispered voice signaled to him. "Hey . . . Over here . . ." A girl was standing not far away, in the center of the cleared path. She was wearing a union suit like his, only hers was striped pink and gray. Her curly dark hair was pulled back in a ponytail, and a black collar of bells hung around her neck. "Don't touch those."

Where had she come from? Could he trust her?

He glanced at the rosebush, then nodded, his face flushing. "I should've known."

"You're new."

James didn't understand what she meant by *new*, but he nodded again anyway.

"Follow me," she said.

"Follow you where?"

"I know how to get out."

"Out?"

She waved him forward. "I'm Lainey."

"James," said James.

"This way." Lainey walked up the path.

They were heading away from the ravine. "Where are we?" he asked.

She sniffed, annoyed. "The Happy Birthday Man Birthday Camp, of course."

"But . . . *how?*"

Her fingers brushed at the collar around her neck. "The bells. I found them in the woods. I put them on. And here I am."

"I found mine in my dresser."

"It's best if we don't talk," she said. "Not until we get to the tent."

The tent?

She waved him forward. They passed half a dozen wildly colored flowers, each made of twisted balloons. Was this the right way? As they walked, more balloons appeared. They weren't only flowers and plants anymore. Giant rubber animals stood behind trees. Each animal was taller than the last. A lime rabbit. A sky-blue tiger. A fuchsia elephant. The rubbery animals squeaked as they turned to watch James and Lainey pass by. He held his breath, too frightened to look back.

Ahead, helium-filled balloons were tethered to strings lining the trail. A meadow opened before them. In the middle of the meadow stood an enormous circus tent, a giant pole pitched in its center, red polka dots marking a stark white canvas. James gaped in awe. Other trails opened onto the clearing too. Kids emerged from the woods, heading toward the tent's open flap. Each wore a union suit of different colors, as well as those insidious black bell collars.

"I thought you said you knew a way out," he said. "This is not *out*."

Lainey continued walking. James held back. He noticed a grand placard across the clearing, near the flap, set upon a thin metal stand. In blood-red ink, calligraphed writing proclaimed: *Meet the Happy Birthday Man! Inside!* But the space beyond the flap was dark. The other kids moved around him, wordlessly passing through the crooked archway as if they'd been here before, as if they all knew exactly what to do.

Lainey grabbed his hand. "You have to trust me."

Inside, wooden bleachers circled a central ring. Lainey directed James up several steps and then parked herself on the bench. Nobody spoke. The bells were their voices now. Echoing in the shadows. The sandy surface of the ring had been raked smooth. The seating area was nearly full, with a few stragglers scrambling to grab open spots. The only ones left were in the front row.

The lights went out. A hushed murmur flitted around the bleachers. James wanted to reach for the girl's hand, but she suddenly seemed very far away. In the dark, a calliope played a familiar tune. "The Birthday Song."

From the far side of the ring, there came a skittering sound, as if something large was being dragged across the sandy floor.

Happy birthday to you . . .

The skittering came again. The ground shivered. The bleachers rocked. James clutched at the bench.

Happy birthday, happy birthday . . .

There was a brief metallic clanging, and then a glaring spotlight illuminated the empty ring. From just outside of the glow, that skittering-scraping sound reverberated.

Happy birthday to you . . .

The calliope music died out. There was a click, and something massive fell from above. James flinched and nearly screamed. Thousands of balloons—the same bright colors he'd noticed while walking through the woods—had been released from a giant net. The crowd gasped.

The balloons began to bounce off a large shape that hadn't been in the ring moments earlier. It stood nearly twenty feet tall. As the last of the balloons sprang away, James clapped his hand over his mouth.

The skin of the creature was decorated like a circus clown—all stripes and dots and colorful pompom-like bumps—but there were also claws and teeth and luminescent scales that changed shade as the thing dragged itself farther into the center of the ring.

The Happy Birthday Man.

Frozen, James watched as it took in the crowd with many great, glossy red eyes. It opened its mouth and roared, flecks of spit spraying across the bleachers. The closest members of the audience were splattered, but not one of them moved.

James's skin felt numb. Lainey sat beside him, shivering.

The Happy Birthday Man slithered forward as the front row leaned backward. The creature zeroed in on one section. A black-and-white-striped appendage swung out toward a small, pale boy who sat wide-eyed and rigid with fear. As its many fingers closed around his torso, the boy made barely a peep; however, when the arm lifted him from the bench, he shrieked. The cry rang through the cavernous space. James could feel it in his veins, his nerves. He recoiled as the Happy Birthday Man brought the boy toward one of its toothy openings. James closed his eyes. The screaming halted. The silence that followed made his muscles shrink onto his bones.

A moment later, to James's surprise, the crowd burst into applause. Cheers! Feet-banging! Whoops and hollers. It was sickening.

James felt the bench drop away beneath him. He was falling.

Falling.

Falling into darkness.

Was this the way out? Was this why the others had cheered?

James jolted awake on his sweat-drenched mattress. He sat up, choking for breath, kicking his damp sheets down to the end of his bed.

He was home.

Home!

It had been a dream. A nightmare. There had been no camp. There had been no Happy Birthday Man. How far back did the dream go? Maybe there had never even been a road, or a path, or that cliff.

James's brain was jumbled. His tongue felt coated in dust (*from the circus ring*). He swung his feet over the edge of the bed (*of the ravine*) and stood up, rushing out to the hallway (*the trail through the woods*) and into the bathroom (*the tent*). He flicked the light switch and bumped his way off the walls toward the sink. He ducked his head down to the faucet. He drank and drank. Looking in the mirror, his breath fogged the glass. His eyes were tired. His skin like ash. A moment later, glittering swimmers, like confetti, filled his vision, and, light-headed, he had to hold on to the sink to keep from falling to the floor. He'd been seeing stars. A moment later, the sparks of light dissipated, but the dizziness remained.

Still, he was grateful beyond words that his brother and sister were asleep just down the hall, that his bed was waiting for him, that he had his headphones and a ton of music to distract himself from the darkness and the things that haunted his mind. Still, he wished his parents were home.

Soon.

Soon.

He was about to turn off the faucet when a noise came from behind him. The shower curtain had been pulled shut, hiding what was in the bathtub. He went stiff. From behind the curtain, the noise came again. Now, he heard it clearly. A bell.

Bells.

His skin prickled.

There was a chiming.

As if from far away.

But this isn't real, he thought.

It's in my head.

Isn't it?

In the dream, Lainey had asked him if he was *new*. Had that meant she'd been to the tent before?

Did it mean he'd end up there again?

Soon.

Soon.

Trembling, James grasped the edge of the shower curtain. Yanking it aside, he didn't have time to gasp.

The bells went *jingle-jangle* . . .

Jingle-jangle . . .

Slowing, like a lullaby before sleep.

AMELIA AND WINTER

Win burst out laughing.

Amelia looked up from the page, confused. "What's wrong with you? You didn't think that was scary?"

"It was mostly funny!" Win replied. "There was a clown!"

"A *monster* clown," Amelia whispered. "Who *ate* a kid."

Defiant, Win crossed his arms. "Clowns are funny."

"What about the other stories? The psycho-killer in a Halloween mask? The ghost looking for revenge? Were those funny too?"

"Hilarious."

"But you didn't read the earlier stories. The one about the Baby Witch who said—"

Said what, Amelia? Do you really want to tell your little brother about the family of witches who can make people disappear? Do you really want to send him down the same spiral that's making you feel almost dizzy with worry?

Win set his jaw. *"Hilarious,"* he repeated, defiantly.

To Amelia the stories were the opposite of hilarious. They had soaked into her pores, chilled her marrow. They had spread beyond the pages of the book, out into the library itself—the bells ringing down the hall, the tapping inside the fireplace, the smell of the exhaust. This wasn't necessarily a bad thing. The stories were addictive—like roller-coaster rides, each one a rush, a race into darkness. She couldn't laugh them away, especially since she couldn't help but feel there was an echo of Grandmother in each, of what may or may not have happened as Grandmother had turned these pages herself. For if there was one thing Amelia's instincts were telling her, it was that Grandmother *had* read the tales. The message on the front page, *DO NOT READ THIS BOOK*, had been Grandmother's handwriting, even if it had only been in a dream. Now, however, Amelia wasn't sure that a dream was *all* it had been. It was becoming increasingly clear that the tales were adding up to something more than just a ride, a race, a rush. Something in them had caused Grandmother to go. To leave. *No.* To disappear.

Amelia flipped back to the beginning. To the story of Moll's Well. It took her a few seconds to locate the right page.

"What are you doing?" Win asked impatiently.

"Hold on," Amelia answered, not looking up. And there it was. A list of the names of the guilty families. The ones who had come for Moll. The Spencers, the Fullers, the Carvers, the Brewsters, the Hathornes, the Winslows, the Martins, and of course Judge Turner. Then, Amelia searched each story. And there they were. Jenny Carver in "The Babysitter and the Bell." Ephraim Winslow in "The Ride." Laura Turner, the ghost girl in "The New House." The cabin in "The Psychopath's Tarot" belonged to a family called the Brewsters. And the other tales seemed connected to the Bowens directly.

Amelia brushed goose bumps from her arms and shook her hair away from her neck.

In her story, the Baby Witch had said something about revenge . . . Was this book a collection of tales about how the Bowens had come for every family who had hurt them, who had forced them from their land, their *legacy*, and had taken what had belonged to them?

Certainly, there was this: Grandmother was a Turner. Married to Grandfather. Who had been a Turner. They had both disappeared. (*DO NOT READ THIS BOOK.*) Amelia was a Turner. So was Winter. (And Mama. Mom too.) If they were to reach the end, would they disappear too?

"AMELIA!" Win shrieked.

She nearly flew up out of her chair in surprise. Slamming the book shut on her lap, she glared at her little brother. "Winter, you have to keep quiet!" she whispered.

"Sor-*ry*," he whined, squirming in his seat.

Amelia flipped through the few dozen pages that were left. "You want to leave?" she asked with defeat. Even though she was frightened of what they might discover next, she *did* want to keep reading. Grandmother felt closer than ever now.

"No!" Win yelled. "More!"

"More?" Amelia was confused. "I thought you didn't like these stories."

"Home is BORING," Win whined. "*Here* is fun. I can hear the jingling bells. The ones from the clown story."

Amelia's spine stiffened. "You heard them too?"

"Yeah. And the girls who were screaming just outside."

She hadn't heard any girls. Maybe she'd been too lost inside the last few stories to notice. Or maybe the screaming she'd imagined while reading "Screamers" hadn't *only* been in her imagination.

"It's like magic in this room," said Win. "I like it. I like being with you." His gap-toothed smile made him look goofy, but it also made him look exactly like himself.

"You do?" Did reading these tales to her brother make her a good big sister? No . . . a *great* big sister? Someone the older kids would want on the yearbook staff at her new school in the fall?

"Mom and Mama won't be done for a long time," said Win. "Can't we stay at least until the library closes?"

Amelia sighed.

A tapping sound came again from the fireplace across the room. Her skin prickled as she thought of the man with the upside-down head. Someone in another part of the library was clomping around in what sounded like thick-soled boots, just like the ones the guy who'd been hiding in that family's closet had worn. A flash of color appeared at the end of the hallway—a bunch of balloons floated at the circulation desk. Had they been there earlier?

If she needed to get to the final page of this book (and she was sure now that she did, despite the risk), wouldn't it be better with her brother beside her? Grandmother didn't *only* belong to Amelia. Grandmother had been part of Win's life as well. When they were done reading, maybe Win would have something to add? Some little-kid insight that pointed toward a detail Amelia might have missed? Something that would lead them to an answer? To Grandmother herself? Or maybe she was just trying to talk herself into continuing.

Looking at the book, Amelia imagined sitting with Win in the front seat of a roller-coaster car, heading up a giant hill—the kind that held you for a moment right before the drop. Mom and Mama would be furious if they knew she'd been reading stories like this to him. Putting him in danger.

(Could stories be dangerous? Well, *yes*, if they made you disappear . . .)

Would that matter if it forced their mothers to understand what had actually happened? Even if the answers felt . . . impossible?

"You win, Win." Amelia smiled.

"Yes!" Win hissed. "What's the next one called?"

STRANGE CLAY

The neighborhood kids had gathered again at the end of the
dead-end street around the corner from Isaac's house, just
like they did every day after school. He listened to them
at his bedroom window. Their shouting, teasing, laughing voices
carried across Mrs. Genovese's backyard just like the cackling of
crows did in the evenings from out in the woods. His father had
told him that they roosted there. The crows. Not the kids. One
day soon, when Isaac's father had the time, they would hike
together and find them—see if they had secrets to share.

His mother peeked in and said, "Go."

"No one likes me," said Isaac.

"They don't know you, honey. Give them a chance."

"I've tried. Gavin Spencer is a bully." When Isaac's family moved to town earlier that year, he'd tried to share his
sketches of dinosaurs and prehistoric megafauna and modern-
day raptor birds with Gavin and Cameron and Jay at school.
They'd laughed him out of the library.

"Gavin Spencer isn't the only one out there. What about Sarah? Or Bobby? You like them, don't you?"

Isaac wouldn't have considered Sarah or Bobby to be *friends*, exactly; however, they'd never called him *Nerd-Boy* or *I-Sick* like Gavin and his best pals did.

"Put on your sneakers," his mother insisted. Isaac groaned. "You can't complain if you don't try." The thing was: Isaac never planned on complaining.

"**Look** who it is!" Gavin cried when he saw Isaac approaching. *Of course* Gavin Spencer was the first to notice him. "What's new, *Nerd-Boy?*"

Isaac raised an eyebrow. "You tell me," he said, trying to bring his voice low like some horrid beast, but sounding instead like a toad with a cold. Gavin laughed and turned to his friends, who whispered as they glared at him.

"Hey there, Isaac," said a voice behind him. It was Bobby. Sarah was beside him. They waved him away from Gavin and the other kids. "Weird seeing you out here."

"It's *nice*, too," said Sarah, throwing Bobby a harsh look.

Isaac felt his face grow warm. He was about to say *My mom made me*, but he caught himself. "I heard the group from my house."

Sarah nodded toward the end of the street, where the asphalt crumbled to dirt and the woods rose up dense and dark, marking the spot where the *end* became *dead*. "Gavin says he found this weird old boulder down in some ravine, and he wants to show everyone."

Gavin Spencer was interested in something other than a video game? "Must be *some* boulder," said Isaac.

"Come with us," Bobby suggested.

Gavin was deep in conversation with his friends now, gesturing toward the trees as if drawing a map through the air with his fingers.

It'll probably be all right, Isaac thought, *if I stick with Bobby and Sarah.*

A few minutes later, Gavin led them into the woods. There were a few other kids Isaac didn't know who lived in different sections of the town and who rode on separate buses to school. He followed along the thin, well-worn trail, up and over several moss-covered, bedrock ridges. They walked on and on—much farther than what felt to Isaac like a half mile.

The forest that hugged their housing development was scattered with enormous chunks of granite, dropped by passing glaciers in an era lost to time. It was hard for Isaac to imagine the mountains of ice that had made the chasms rough and then smoothed the walls of rock. Sometimes Isaac hiked with his father back here. He'd bring along his sketchbook, and they'd pause whenever Isaac noticed a leaf or a tree or a mushroom he thought was beautiful, his father whistling while Isaac pressed the tip of his pencil against the paper, conjuring in a few quick marks what Isaac felt was the spirit of the object. Despite what he'd been taught in catechism, Isaac believed that *everything* on this planet had a soul—or if not a soul exactly, then an energy that made it worth capturing, at least on the page.

The group reached a spot he had never seen before—a deep gouge in the earth, like a mini crater from a fallen meteorite. The kids stood at its edge. "There," Gavin said, pointing at the center, where an enormous rock sat half buried in a thick blanket of dead leaves. Unlike the other chunks of stone they'd passed on their hike through the woods, this boulder was pure white. As they all edged down the slope, Isaac felt a thrumming inside his rib cage, as if the alabaster boulder were singing or humming, whispering important instructions that Isaac couldn't make out. The kids were whispering too, shocked at the rock's bizarre appearance. They spread out and made their way down. Isaac walked with Bobby and Sarah. Everyone gawped as Gavin Spencer cackled, proud of himself. "I think I'll call it Gavin's Rock."

The boulder was a few inches taller than Isaac himself, so pale that it gleamed, even in the shadow of the forest's canopy. It looked wet, covered in glob-like bumps, but when Isaac brushed his hand against it, his fingertips came away dry.

"The strangest part," Gavin whispered. He pointed to a gap where the boulder met the blanket of leaves. It looked like an animal burrow. "You know about nature stuff, *Nerd-Boy*," Gavin said. Isaac flinched. "What's inside?"

"No clue," he answered.

"Want to find out?" Gavin asked. The others tittered. The thing was, Isaac *did* want to find out. That singing, humming, whispering in his head went on. "Reach in. I dare you."

His mother's voice came to him, giving encouragement about friendship and trying new experiences, even when they made him nervous. "Fine," said Isaac, kneeling beside the hole. Maybe this would make them realize he wasn't a *Nerd-Boy* after all.

A smell wafted forth. If this were an animal den, there would be an aroma of waste and sweat and birth. Instead came the smell of char. And damp earth. Old ice. Mildew. If he stuck his hand inside, nothing would bite. He was almost positive.

Almost.

As his arm slid into the hole, he felt the temperature change. Inside was dank, filled with a needle-like chill. The group murmured behind him, shocked at his bravery. He was shocked too. When his shoulder was nearly at the mouth of the hole, and his torso pressed to the ground, his fingers touched a soft substance. There was some give to it, like *clay*—the kind in art class that came in big rectangular slabs, wrapped in plastic to keep it from drying out. Curious, Isaac forced his fingers into the substance, pulled off a piece of it, and clutched it in his fist.

Something grabbed at his belt. Frantic, he yanked himself away from the hole.

The group laughed, even Bobby and Sarah, their voices echoing out into the woods like animals set loose from a cage. Gavin Spencer was crouched beside Isaac, guffawing so hard he looked like he couldn't breathe. "Holy heck, *Nerd-Boy*, you should have seen yourself jump!"

Isaac scrambled to his feet, warmth coming back into his arm. Had the whole hike been a joke?

Gavin caught his breath. "Dude, you are *such* a loser."

Isaac glared at Bobby and Sarah, who were suddenly sheepish. Breaking through the line of kids, he raced out of the ravine. They shouted at him.

Don't be so sensitive . . .

Only a joke . . .

Being called loser *is not a joke*, he thought. He ran through the woods and didn't stop until he reached the broken asphalt at the dead end. The corner of his street was up ahead. His temples burned, and he gritted his teeth, holding back rage.

Something felt heavy in his hand. Opening his fist, he saw an oblong shape. The thing *was* clay, straight from the earth itself. Like the rock that had been hiding it, the glob was pure white. Creases from his skin were captured in its surface.

At home, Isaac smashed his face into his pillow so his mother couldn't hear his sobs.

You don't get to complain if you don't try.

After a quiet dinner, he sat at his desk by the window. The sky darkened over the jagged line of trees. He examined the glob. Isaac thought of the jolt that had rocked his body when Gavin Spencer had grabbed him, of how he'd wanted to melt when the other kids had laughed and pointed. He pressed his thumb into the center of the white lump, creating a tiny version of the crater in the woods.

An unfinished sketch of a toadstool stared up from his open notebook. Isaac moved the clay between his palms until it had formed a small roll. He flattened one end of it and broke a piece off the other and used that to shape a sort of soft pyramid. A mushroom cap. He placed the cap on the end of the roll, smoothing the clay at the joint, then compared the sculpture to the sketch in his notebook.

Holding the clay, he experienced something similar to the thrumming sensation he'd felt earlier—like a vibration in his brain. Dragging his fingernail down the bottom of the cap, he thought of Gavin Spencer's smug face. The mark he left looked like a gaping mouth. He added empty holes for eyes, then pinched away two pieces of clay and made long, reaching arms. Placing the sculpture on his desk, he leaned back in his chair and admired the mushroom creature. It howled silently at him.

As he slipped under his covers, a crescent moon was just

peeking over the trees near the dead end. He closed his eyes, thinking of how the clay had shifted between his fingers.

When the moon had traveled a little over halfway across the sky, a sound woke Isaac with a start. Sitting, he heard it again. A booming crash. A shuddering echo.

It had come from outside.

Isaac kicked away his blankets. He looked to the woods. Some of the trees were swaying, but there was no wind. A large pine jolted to one side, then toppled with a house-shaking wallop. Isaac saw something large moving through the forest. Two pale appendages reached for the indigo clouds.

Isaac glanced at the white mushroom creature on his desk.

Crash-BOOM! Another tree cracked, shook the ground.

He brought his hand down on top of his sculpture. The clay smooshed beneath his palm.

Outside, the night went silent.

Whatever had been there was gone.

In the morning, Isaac went into the woods. About two hundred feet from where his backyard ended, four pines had fallen. Their thick trunks were twisted like broken bodies, bark skin bulging, innards splintering outward.

He made it to the bus stop just as the driver was about to pull away. He ignored Bobby and Sarah and Gavin Spencer and sat near the back. As the bus bumped over the cracked pavement, Isaac wondered if anyone else had seen the creature the night before, or if it had only been him. He sure as heck wasn't going to ask.

During classes, Isaac's mind kept coming back to the boulder and the clay, to the pale giant and the fallen trees. At lunch, Isaac snuck to the art room and asked Mr. Hesse about where the clay in the ceramics studio came from. "All my classes are full for the quarter," the teacher answered. "Try again next year." That wasn't what Isaac wanted to know, but from Mr. Hesse's expression, he understood that the teacher was done with him.

Frustrated, he sought his science instructor and asked what she knew about alabaster stone. Ms. Frommer gave him a quizzical look and then pointed toward the classroom bookshelf. "If you're looking to do some extra credit, let me know what you find."

By the time he climbed off the bus that afternoon, doubt bubbled in his brain. What if those four pines he'd discovered that morning had been busted already? What if all of this was only in his head? Thankfully, there was a way to find out. At home, Isaac rushed upstairs. The pancake slab of white clay was dried out on his desk. As he tried to bend it, the clay crumbled. Undeterred, he grabbed half a dozen plastic sandwich baggies from a kitchen drawer, shoved them into the pockets of his jacket, and headed out the back door.

Outside, Isaac heard the neighborhood kids from across Mrs. Genovese's yard. They'd already gathered at the dead end. Behind his house, Isaac stepped into the woods and hiked up the hill. A bedrock trail curled toward a familiar-looking ridge.

By the time Isaac reached the crater, his stomach felt funny. As soon as he allowed his gaze to fix on the white rock, that singing, humming, whispering sound haunted the deep end of his mind. Today, the rock glowed brighter than before.

Isaac laid the plastic baggies on the ground. That same smell emanated from the hole—smoke, ash, and the damp tang of minerals. He held his breath as he ducked down and shoved his arm into the hole again. Again and again, he clasped pieces of clay, pulling them out of the darkness, and sealed them inside the baggies. When he was done, he sat on his heels, coated in sweat. Crows squawked from above. They'd been watching like little judges.

He didn't expect to find his mother waiting eagerly for him in the kitchen. "Were you out with the kids again?"

"Yup," Isaac lied. "They're not as bad as I thought they'd be."

"I'm proud of you, honey," she said. "Go wash up. Dinner will be ready in a few. Hope you're in the mood for mac and cheese."

"Always!" Isaac said, forcing cheer. What he was really in the mood for was the white clay in his pockets.

Later, Isaac sat at his desk as the sky turned violet. He'd opened two of the plastic baggies and combined their contents, making a lump of clay that was twice as large as the one he'd used the night before. Flipping through his sketchbook, he came upon a small box turtle that he'd found out in the woods with his father over the summer. There was a soft gleam in its eyes. Isaac molded the clay, shaping four legs, a head, a tail, and the dome of a shell that matched the patterns on the sketched turtle's back. He paid attention to the details of his drawing, trying to capture the gentleness he'd observed in the real animal's gaze. Using his fingernails, he carved lumps and wrinkles to create delicate yet rough-looking skin. He placed the turtle on the ledge in front of the window, as the moon, a bit fuller than it had been yesterday, peeked up over the horizon. Feeling strangely satisfied, he went downstairs to watch television with his parents.

In the night, a cracking resounded from outside. As he'd waited nervously for this moment, Isaac's mind did not allow him to sleep. Now, he flung his blankets aside with excitement. At the window, he saw the tops of the trees wavering against the rising constellations. A warmth rushed through him. His turtle sat just where he had left it on the ledge. Isaac squinted at the forest. If there was something out there, it wasn't tall enough to break through the canopy. Slipping into jeans and a sweater, he took the sculpture off the sill, crept downstairs, and grabbed a flashlight from a drawer in the hallway. At the back door, he put on his jacket and sneakers and then eased himself outside, down the steps, across the patio, and into the yard.

He marched across the grass, frost crunching under his feet. An ambient quiet vibrated his eardrums. At the edge of the woods, he listened for something louder. Soon came the *swoosh-woosh* of branches whipping high up, followed by tree trunks groaning as they swayed toward their breaking points. Something was moving through the night. Something large.

The clay sculpture felt heavy in Isaac's hands, and for a moment, he sensed a throbbing inside it like a heartbeat, but then he realized it was his blood rushing though his own veins.

He flicked on the flashlight and pointed it into the woods, the pale spot brushing across saplings. "Hello?" Isaac whispered, not wanting to startle the creature.

When he reached the crest of the hill, a gigantic pale dome appeared several dozen yards ahead. Isaac's skin went all gooseflesh. He focused the flashlight beam down the incline, but the glow didn't quite reach. There was a shuffling and a grating noise as if tough skin were scraping against tree bark.

Soon, the flashlight lit a mass of white. An enormous eye blinked. Isaac nearly fell over. There was no pupil or iris—just a blank, milky glaze. The ground trembled as the creature shied from the light. Isaac lowered it. "Sorry," he called out. "Don't go. Please."

It was still for a moment before bringing its massive head forward again.

Isaac couldn't believe what he was seeing. It was a turtle, *his* turtle—the one he'd made out of clay—and it was bigger than his house. Like the boulder, its body was pure white and shiny, like tumbled stones. Isaac edged closer, holding out his hand. The turtle was right before him. Its nostrils flared. A rush of cold breath hit Isaac in the face, and he laughed in disbelief. He brought his palm to its flesh. Life pulsed against his skin.

He felt a pressure welling up behind his eyes, and he suddenly felt foolish for getting teary in front of the giant turtle.

"Look," Isaac said, holding out the sculpture for the animal to see. "It's you."

The creature's eyes flashed. Its neck jutted backward into its shell.

"Wait! I'm sorry. That was dumb of me."

But it was too late. The turtle's substantial skull retracted fully. Then it pulled its arms and legs inside too.

"You don't have to be scared," Isaac pleaded. "I'm your friend." A soft groan came from inside the shell, and he knew it was over.

Isaac sat for a while, staring at the bundled creature, but soon, a chill penetrated his jacket. As he made his way up the slope, he peered over his shoulder. But the creature only continued to sit, tucked away from the world, newly born and fearful.

Exhausted, Isaac woke late. His mother rushed him out the door. He had brought the sculpture wrapped in plastic with him onto the bus, holding it in his hands, hoping Mr. Hesse would let him fire it in the classroom kiln.

"What does *Nerd-Boy* have today?" As Isaac passed him, Gavin Spencer stood and followed. "Some kind of science project?"

"You know the rules, boys," said the driver. "Sit now, or we sit here."

Isaac plopped down in the second-to-last row. Gavin blocked him in. "Turtle got your tongue?"

Bobby and Sarah were several rows ahead. Neither looked back. A tightness crept in from the edges of Isaac's vision. He knew this feeling. Rage. It made him feel out of control, like an animal. He imagined being able to pull his head down inside his torso and hide away from the things that scared him or that made him angry. He considered how some turtles lash out instead—their mouths quick sharp machines.

Gavin Spencer grabbed the sculpture from Isaac's lap and stood. "Look what *Nerd-Boy* made!" he called out. "Godzilla's turtle buddy, Gamera!"

"It's not Gamera!" Isaac cried. Bobby and Sarah and the other kids on the bus were all staring now.

"Gavin!" the driver yelled. "Sit down!"

But Gavin only laughed harder. Isaac lunged. Gavin whipped the turtle aside. The plastic wrap slipped, and the sculpture flew from Gavin's grasp. It hit the back of the seat one row up, then fell to the floor. The driver slammed on the brakes and Gavin tumbled forward, landing directly on top of it.

"I said park it!" the driver called again.

By now, the rest of the bus was laughing at Gavin, who was peeling himself up off the aisle. Isaac focused instead on the smashed clay beneath him.

If the turtle had still been out in the woods that morning, surely, it was gone now.

At school, the principal gave Gavin Spencer detention. It wasn't for what he'd done to Isaac, but for not listening when the driver had told him to sit.

Throughout the day, Isaac could think of nothing but the few sealed bags of wet clay that were resting on his desk at home.

"Gavin Spencer is so awful," Sarah said at lunch.

"What a jerk," Bobby agreed.

"We're gonna hang out at the dead end today," Sarah said. "You should come."

Isaac had been staring stone-faced at the wall. "I'd . . . like that."

"Bobby's going to teach me how to do an ollie. Do you skate?"

"Not yet," said Isaac. He was surprised how easy it was to shove all his anger and fear into a hole deep inside himself.

"It takes practice," said Bobby. "And a few bruises. But I bet you're tougher than you look."

"I bet I am too," Isaac answered.

That afternoon, Isaac walked with Bobby and Sarah to the dead end. He tried Bobby's skateboard, centering himself and pushing along the cracked asphalt before tumbling onto the grass at the edge of the road. When Bobby and Sarah laughed, he laughed along with them. *Try new things*, he heard his mother's voice in his head.

New things . . .

As the sun sank behind the trees, casting long shadows across the neighborhood lawns, a Gavin-shaped figure appeared at the end of the block. When the boy approached, Isaac asked the question he'd been planning since lunchtime, just after Bobby and Sarah had invited him to hang out at the dead end. "Do you two want to see what I found last night?"

"Sure," said Bobby. "Where?"

"Out in the woods. Too big to bring home."

"What is it?" Sarah asked.

"You should come too, Gavin," Isaac answered. "I bet it'll blow your mind."

"Oh, you *bet*?" Gavin Spencer sneered, then chuckled. When Sarah and Bobby didn't respond, Gavin kicked a stone.

"Let's meet at midnight," Isaac said to Bobby and Sarah. "Right here. Bring flashlights."

A stab of fear opened Sarah's eyes wider. *"Midnight?"*

"Don't tell me you guys are actually going to do this," Gavin went on. "It's obviously a trick, to get back at me for this morning."

"To get back at you for what?" If Gavin wasn't going to apologize, Isaac wanted at least to hear him admit what he'd done.

"Whatever, dude. You two are chumps if you take whatever this kid's serving up."

"But *we* didn't do anything to Isaac," said Sarah, raising an eyebrow.

Exactly, thought Isaac. *You didn't do* anything.

"We'll be here," said Bobby with a wink. "Midnight."

At dinner, Isaac ate quietly as his parents talked about their day. Afterward, he washed his hands, then went to his room. Checking the clock, he opened the last of the plastic baggies and got to work.

Mom and Dad's television went quiet at around eleven o'clock. Isaac sat on his bed, his spine pressed against the wall as he stared out at the night sky.

Soon, it was time to go. Tonight, he dressed extra warm. He left the new sculpture on his windowsill; no way he was going to let Gavin smash it. When Isaac reached the dead end, he noticed several beams of light. He waved his own light over his head.

The group was larger than he'd anticipated. There was Bobby and Sarah. Gavin Spencer's curiosity had gotten the better of him. His fear must have gotten him too, because he'd brought along his best pals, Cameron and Jay. "This had better be good," Gavin said.

In the darkness, Isaac felt bold. "And if it's not?" he shot back.

"Just . . . watch yourself."

"I'd say the same to you," Isaac added. "The woods are trickier at night." Cameron and Jay chuckled. Gavin threw them a glare. "Everyone ready?" Sarah and Bobby said yes, so Isaac led the way. Up the hill. Across the bedrock. The flashlights bounced manically around the trail.

"You're taking us back to the boulder?" asked Sarah once they'd reached the first crest.

In the distance, there was a booming crash. The ground shook. A group of roosting crows took flight, filling the night with wild chatter.

Isaac felt a hand clasp his arm. Sarah was at his side. "This way." He waved everyone forward.

Gavin Spencer held back. "I don't think—"

But Isaac ignored his plea. He headed into the brush, kicking at the carpet of rotting leaves. He wanted his clay avatar to hear them coming.

"You're sure it's safe out here?" asked Bobby.

"As safe as skateboarding," Isaac said with a smile. "You'll be fine. I bet you're tougher than you look." He took them up and down the rocky slopes. Then, in a clearing ahead, he saw it, illuminated by the waxing moon. He sensed an enormous set of eyes zeroing in on them. "Over here," he whispered.

Sarah gasped. The others froze, and focused their flashlights forward. Gavin's voice rose an octave. "What is that?"

He was answered by a roar that shattered the night.

An alabaster tyrannosaur dipped its head down as it raised its tail, showing sixty perfectly sculpted white razor-sharp teeth. Isaac stood in awe as his friends fell backward, tripping over themselves to get out of the way. The dinosaur's muscles rippled underneath scaly pearlescent skin. Claws clicked as meaty legs brought its massive feet closer. Isaac couldn't look away. This was the most beautiful thing he'd ever seen.

And he'd built it. Which made him . . . what? A god? He chuckled at the thought.

"Isaac!" Sarah called from up the slope. "Run!"

Isaac turned to see that most of the group was already racing off. He pursued them. The ground trembled as the dinosaur gave chase, knocking through the trees. Looking back, Isaac saw wide roots tip upward as the earth opened underneath them.

Another roar tore through the woods, and the kids screamed in response. Isaac felt like laughing, but he was running too fast and his breath was short. He raced ahead of his creation. He wanted to roar, to scare his tormentors out of the woods and out of their minds. He wanted his voice to carry across the night, to rouse the sleeping neighborhood and make them wonder.

He dashed up the hill, cold breath whooshing at his back. His sneaker caught on a root, and Isaac fell forward, landing in a pile of pine needles. Pain bloomed in his forehead and in his palms. The bedrock quaked so hard, Isaac worried it might split open and eat him up. But the beast's footfalls diminished as it chased the screaming kids toward the bluestone trail.

"Wait . . . ," Isaac groaned. "Wait for me." When he reached for the flashlight, he noticed his hands were dark with blood. "Sarah! Bobby!" he called out. But no one answered. He limped up the hill. From far ahead came sounds of breaking branches, thick calluses padding, and claws scraping up the ground. At the crest, the trail was laid out before him. The others were gone. They'd made it out of the woods. For a moment, Isaac felt the familiar tightness at the edge of his vision, that ache in the back of his skull. The rage. The anger.

He'd wanted to see their fear.

A great hissing erupted from the bottom of the hill. A bulk of white was heading toward him. The creature was returning. Isaac thought of the giant turtle from the night before, how gentle it had been before he'd frightened it. His new creation's head hung low, its tail stretched out far behind its torso, balancing its weight. Closer it came. Closer. It looked defeated. As defeated as Isaac felt. He stood and held out his hand. He knew the creature wouldn't shy away from him like the great turtle had done the previous night. This one was bolder. Stronger. More clever. Just like Isaac would be from now on.

The white tyrannosaur tromped back along its path of destruction. Isaac smiled as it approached. Cold seeped through his coat, but he barely noticed. His hand, still outstretched, was slick. Only several yards away now, the creature bowed. Its neck extended. Its massive skull was near enough for Isaac to touch. An icy sensation met his palm.

Isaac's body flushed with a strange feeling, and he imagined himself glowing from within. There was that humming sound again, that whispering, singing. A melody twirling through the night, spiraling between the broken tree trunks, fueled by darkness and starlight. This was power, Isaac knew. This was what Gavin Spencer woke up feeling every single morning. Isaac never wanted it to go away.

He wanted this moment to last forever.

The tyrannosaur jolted backward, the dark spot of Isaac's blood on the tip of its snout. For a moment, its white eyes seemed to flash black, and Isaac finally felt the night's cold deep in his gut. The beast opened its mouth. It let out a sound like angry angels screaming. Its breath was a winter wind, so strong that it whipped Isaac's hair away from his face. In awe, Isaac directed the flashlight upward.

There was red on the creature's teeth. Again, those dull white eyes glinted a clever black.

Had the others made it out of the woods?

The creature lunged.

"No! Stop!" Isaac shouted.

Its jaws snapped with a violent clack. And a crunch. And then, a gulp.

A gentle breeze rustled the leaves.

Soon, the crows that had been disturbed returned to find their roosting tree was toppled. Their numbers rose as they gathered on other branches instead. Their chatter swelled. It turned out, they had some new secrets to share.

THE VOLUNTEERS

From the files of Miles Holiday
The Offices of Invisible Intelligence, LLC

Dear Layne,

I came across an interesting case.

The Martin family went missing in the summer of 1979. Finn and Kaitlyn were parents to Agatha and Benjamin. Their disappearance was a big mystery at the time. The story made national news. Do you remember? It's still unsolved.

The house was untouched. The car was in the garage. But the family? Gone, gone, gone.

I've unearthed a diary from the youngest son, Benjamin — who was ten at the time of his disappearance — which recounts some strange happenings over the course of the previous nine months. Fascinating stuff. Highly unlikely that any of it is "true." His entries read like they're bursting from a ripening imagination, but they also seem to indicate that *something* happened to the family, even if he's exaggerating whatever it was.

I'm forwarding a copy of his journal to you. Would you mind sending me your thoughts? Maybe *Invisible Intelligence* could do a segment on the mystery of the missing Martins. Clementine and I could talk to some of the neighbors, maybe even see if Benny's best friend, Nico, is still around. I'm sure he'd give a great interview.

Heck, maybe we'll even turn up a few ghosts to hunt.

Let me know. I'd like to begin research as soon as possible.

Yours,

Miles

From the diary of Benjamin Martin:

Sunday, October 15, 1978

Today, something really cool happened. When we got home from church, I found four big pumpkins sitting right in the middle of our porch. They were white and tall and heavy. Mom said, "One for each of us!" Then she picked up a note that had been pinned underneath one. Here it is:

FOR YOUR JACK-O'-LANTERNS.
HAPPY OCTOBER!

A gift from a stranger! I asked Dad if we could carve the jack-o'-lanterns this evening, but he said he was too busy. Mom too. Aggie said she'd help, but she wants to wait for Mom and Dad, and that's okay with me. It's fun to do these things together, I guess. I've already started my design. It's going to have crazy mean eyes and sharp teeth. Like this:

For Halloween this year, I'm going as a pirate. I have an old pair of shorts that I'll cut the bottoms so they look all jagged like how pirates in cartoons wear their pants. Plus there's my red-and-white-striped T-shirt and this old yellow vest from a suit that Granddad left us. And I've got an eyepatch and a bandanna. My best friend, Nico, says he'll go as my parrot, which I think is hilarious. I wonder if we can figure out a way for him to sit on my shoulder.

Tonight, I've been at my bedroom window, watching for a car or two to slow down and notice the four pumpkins sitting on the steps. I'm hoping it'll give us a clue who left the pumpkins for us. The porch light is still shining like a spotlight on them. Since Dad and Mom moved us up into these hills last summer, there's not been a lot of traffic. We don't have many neighbors. Who knows, maybe our secret friend will knock in the middle of the night to say hi.

I cannot wait for Halloween.

Monday, October 16, 1978

Tonight's the full moon! It's so bright out, you can see your shadow. I tried for a little while in the backyard, but then I heard noises in the woods and I ran inside. I didn't tell Aggie I was scared because I knew she'd make fun of me. She's been on the phone all evening with her soccer friends, and those girls can be super mean!

Mom just yelled at Aggie for clogging up the line, but Aggie closed the door in her face. Unbelievable . . . Mom is way too nice sometimes.

I asked around at school, but nobody admitted leaving the pumpkins. Nico said that maybe it was the witches out in the woods and I said yeah right and he raised an eyebrow and got all serious, but even though he's told me stories and legends about this town, I just can't get on board with believing in a family of witches that everyone says used to live around here.

Witches. Ha-ha . . .

Friday, October 20, 1978

Home from Aggie's game. Her team won for the third time in a row! I sat with Nico on the sidelines, and we cheered every time Aggie ran by. I think I noticed her smiling a couple times, so it was worth it. Dad says if the girls keep it up, they'll be heading to the championships for sure.

To celebrate, we went out for pizza with Aggie's team. We ordered a large pie with pepperoni, meatballs, and extra cheese, and guess what? There were no leftovers. Not even one piece.

My stomach hurts.

Monday, October 23, 1978

The whole weekend went by, and I forgot to ask Mom and Dad to help me carve the pumpkins! They were working. Dad says his deadline is going to keep him in the studio full-time for the next few weeks. And Mom's been fielding calls from an emergency at her hospital. Some kind of outbreak, I think? Scary. Oh well . . . At least we have a few more days before Halloween creeps up on us.

Wednesday, October 25, 1978

I found this weird bump on my arm. It's super itchy. I hope I'm not allergic to mosquitoes. Mom says it's late in the season for those. Still, she put this sticky pink lotion on it. It's really smelly and it makes my skin feel all tight.

I have lots of homework tonight. How many maps of the world's countries can one class draw over the course of a single school year? I doubt I'll be able to concentrate. The itch is strong, Obi-Wan.

Friday, October 27, 1978

The rash is all over my arms and neck. The doctor says it's poison ivy. It's so itchy and gross, and when I scratch it, which I'm not supposed to do, it oozes this yellowy gunk. Mom says that the rash is <u>weeping</u>, which I think sounds MUCH worse than oozing.

I know how I got it. I was picking at some plants that were wrapped around the fence at the edge of the recess yard earlier in the week. So stupid. Aggie won't come near me even though Mom says it's not contagious. I keep trying to hug her anyway, just to make her scream.

Sunday, October 29, 1978

My whole body is so itchy I could jump out of my skin. The ooze has spread up to my face. It's in my eyes and my nose and on my lips. Everything is swollen, and I can barely move. Mom says I might not even be able to go trick-or-treating with Nico this week!

Too bad because I already look like a <u>monster</u>.

This is the worst thing that's EVER HAPPENED EVER.

I wish I could leave my body until this is all over. The doctor gave me a pill to take. A steroid, I think. Does this mean I'm going to grow huge muscles like Lou Ferrigno on <u>The Incredible Hulk</u>?

Tuesday, October 31, 1978

It's a sad, stupid Halloween. I've been home from school for the past two days. Thankfully, the medicine is starting to help. I'm "weeping" less. I must still look like a ghoul because even Aggie's been really nice. She decided to watch scary movies with me tonight instead of going out with her friends. Nico said he'll give me half of his candy, which is really cool of him. Still, I feel bad that he's stuck being a big dumb bird all by himself. What's a parrot costume without its pirate?

I can't even cry because one of my eyes is crusted nearly shut. Dad's been working nonstop. And Mom says she hasn't even had time to go out and get candy in case we happen to get any trick-or-treaters. Which, let's be honest, is highly unlikely, since Upper Yarrow Road is in the middle of nowhere.

Those pumpkins are still sitting on the porch. Maybe Aggie will want to carve them later when we're watching <u>Carnival of Souls</u>, but I'm not in the mood anymore. It hurts to even write this.

<u>Wednesday, November 1, 1978</u>

It's the weirdest thing. I woke up this morning feeling much better. I had this strange urge to check the pumpkins on the front stoop. When I went outside, I found them all gray and squishy with their middles caving in. It must have happened overnight, because they definitely didn't look like that yesterday.

I showed them to Dad, and he shoveled them one by one into the backyard. He said the squirrels will have a field day with them come winter. Which I guess is fine, because whenever we have a field day at school, it's always a fun time. I like sack races best. Mom says I should be good to go by the end of the week, but I'm not so sure, since I still look like a freak-and-a-half.

****Note from Miles Holiday:

Layne,

Benjamin's next mention of anything out of the ordinary comes months later, on July 4, 1979.

I have cut the entries that tell of his return to school after the poison ivy, of Agatha's soccer championship win, of Finn finishing his book's illustrations, of Kaitlyn's promotion at the hospital. Benjamin goes into detail about the presents he received for Christmas, about the long drive to visit grandparents in the next state over, about writing an essay for the local newspaper regarding the new skate park outside of town, about his life in general.

I wonder if the boy's strange account may hint at either the return—or worsening—of his autumn illness, or if his writings may be a method of coping with some kind of shock that he is unable—or unwilling—to document here. Are these final few entries his attempt to escape into a fantasy world, albeit a nightmarish one, or could he be using metaphor to describe the reality of some horrible situation? To get a better sense of what might have *actually* happened to the Martins, and to answer the question of why and to where they disappeared, I will need to find context in writings or notations of the other family members.

Whatever the case, except for the gap of seven months, I have made no further modifications to the accounting of the events of summer 1979. It reads as I found it.

From the diary of Benjamin Martin:

Wednesday, July 4, 1979

Last night, there was a bad storm. The thunder was booming like fireworks. In fact, that's what I thought they were at first because our neighbors have been setting them off all week long. The 4th of July and all that. But then I heard the wind and the rain and saw lightning through my curtains. I called for Aggie, because her room's right next to mine, and usually she's as nervous about thunderstorms as I am. (Don't tell Nico, ha-ha.) We've almost always waited them out together in one of our bedrooms, hiding under the covers.

But Aggie didn't answer. So I ducked into my closet and closed the door, and then put my pillow over my head to cover my ears and block out the noise. I must have fallen asleep, because the next thing I knew someone was knocking on the closet door.

At first, I had no idea where I was, because it was so dark, and I was sitting up against the wall, and my winter boots were pressing into my hip. The knocking came again.

After a few seconds, I figured it must have been morning, and that when my mom didn't see me in bed, she checked my closet. The knocking got louder and harder.

I swung open the door. But Mom wasn't there. No one was. The sunlight shined through the curtains. The storm had passed.

I think that maybe I dreamed it. The knocking. Not the storm.

I wonder if I should tell anyone. But then I'd have to admit I spent most of the night sleeping in my closet with my pillow over my head like a dink.

Saturday, July 7, 1979

Me and Nico rode our bikes this afternoon. We must have gone miles because <u>boy are my legs sore</u>! We kept seeing signs for <u>Nite Crawlers</u> posted up and down the road that leads to town. Worms for fishing bait. Nico asked me why they spelled it <u>Nite</u> instead of <u>Night</u>. I realized I have no clue.

When I got home, Mom pointed out these weird-looking plants that had grown up next to the house. She said they looked like the beginnings of pumpkin vines. After Dad dumped the old pumpkins from last fall out near the woods, the squirrels must have burrowed inside and scattered the seeds around the yard. How funny is that? Mom called the vines VOLUNTEERS, since they've decided to grow up in our garden all on their own. She says we'll leave them in, just to see how they do.

I think that's kind of cool. <u>Volunteer pumpkin vines</u> . . . Maybe some pumpkins will even show up!

<u>Monday, July 16, 1979</u>

Here is what the flowers on the pumpkin vines look like:

They're really strange. The flowers bud and then bloom only once, early in the mornings. After that, the big petals curl in on themselves and droop down. The bees have been flocking to the flowers when they're open, hopping from one to the other. Mom says that's how the plants pollinate. After the bees are done, the base of the flower bulges. Mom says the bulges will eventually grow fat. The petals will die and fall away. And then there will be an honest-to-goodness pumpkin. I can't wait. Maybe we can use them for Halloween <u>this</u> year, since last year was such a bust.

Tuesday, July 17, 1979

Last night, I heard someone tapping on my bedroom door. I got up to check, but no one was there. Then I heard knocking downstairs. I was scared to go look but I did it anyway, peeking through the curtain near the front door. No one was there either. Then, it came from the back door. I freaked out and woke up Mom and Dad. They checked, but they couldn't see anyone out there either, even after they turned on the big spotlight on the back deck.

What we could see were the volunteers. The vines are growing like crazy, like they're trying to take over. Nico is coming to see them this afternoon. We're going to help Mom redirect the vines along the edges of the garden so we can still play ball in the yard.

<u>Wednesday, July 18, 1979</u>

This morning, I woke up because Aggie was yelling. I ran downstairs to see what was wrong. Looking outside, I noticed that the vines we moved yesterday had grown back where they were before. And worse! Some of them have climbed onto the deck and are clinging to the house. They have these little tendrils that spiral around and around, searching for something to twist up on and hold tight, kind of like a boa constrictor.

The pollinated flowers have bulged out. White pumpkins are here, growing faster than we thought they would. Dad thinks it's funny. He says we need to tear out at least half the vines. Mom said it's funny that he can't get up out of his chair to help. Absolutely hilarious, but I don't hear anyone laughing.

(Later) This afternoon, me and Mom and Aggie pulled out the vines that were closest to the house. We left the ones that were farther out back. It made me sad, because underneath the wide leaves, we noticed that some of the pumpkins were getting big. We saved them and set them up on the back deck, but we dragged their vines out to the tree line and made a pile. Who knew that stray pumpkin seeds could cause so much trouble?

<u>Thursday, July 19, 1979</u>

Those tapping sounds came again last night. I didn't get out of bed. I almost hid in my closet, but then I remembered what happened last time.

(Later) The vines we pulled out yesterday came back again. I didn't know that plants grew this quickly. Dad's worried about them getting into the house. We found a few tendrils climbing into the dryer vent. When Mom got home from work, we went around the whole yard and yanked every vine we could find.

Afterward, I wanted to ride my bike down to Nico's house, but Dad said it was too dark already and he didn't trust the drivers on Upper Yarrow Road and I asked WHAT DRIVERS? because no one ever comes up here and he got mad and sent me to my room. So that's where I am.

I'm going to read a book since the TV's downstairs, and I'm nowhere near tired yet. I just need to pick the right one. Maybe something scary that I've already read . . . Those books are the best.

<u>Friday, July 20, 1979</u>

It's already evening, and I'm just now able to write this down. If you're reading this—AND WHY WOULD YOU BE READING THIS? IT'S PRIVATE—you probably aren't going to believe what I'm about to say. But it's true. All of this is happening. For real. Somehow.

This morning, I heard a commotion downstairs. I knew what was going on before I got halfway down the stairs because I could see the pumpkin vines from there. They were stretched across the kitchen floor, their leaves already as big as the ones that had been growing outside for the past week. The bright yellow flowers were open, as if waiting for bees to crawl inside.

I found Dad and Mom and Aggie searching for spots where the vines had found their way into our house. It felt like a game. Somehow, one tendril had managed to squeeze through the tiniest gap in the back door. Another had come in through a hole in the screen in the kitchen window. Some had even come through the air vent in the downstairs bathroom.

I asked Dad if we should call the police, and he said he didn't think this was the kind of thing they handled. He reached out to the garden center near the highway instead and told them what was going on. Their advice was to dig up every vine at the root. Then, get this, they said to douse the soil there with a bit of gasoline and set it on fire!

So, after we managed to cut and drag all the new vines out to the woods, that's what we did . . .

All of this has me thinking of the poison ivy on the chain-link fence at school last fall, right before Halloween. Is this like some kind of revenge for plucking at their vines?

Do plants have thoughts and wishes and emotions? Like anger? And fear? Tomorrow, I'm going to ride down to the library to find out.

Hopefully, Nico will tag along. My family is starting to drive me nutty.

<u>Saturday, July 21, 1979</u>

Okay, this is bad. This is very, very bad.

I'm not even sure that I'm <u>not</u> dreaming. I've been pinching myself over and over, and if this <u>is</u> a dream then there are dream-welts up and down my arms.

It's Saturday morning. I think. An hour ago, Mom and Dad knocked on my bedroom door looking weird. They were holding flashlights. Aggie was standing behind them, chewing her lip. The house was dark, and when I tried to flip the light switch, nothing happened.

I asked, What's going on?

They went to my window. Mom pulled back the blinds. The glass was covered by green tendrils, leaves, and those spiky vines. I watched the tendrils moving, twirling in that way I've seen them do in the backyard, searching for something to grab. They're blocking out the daylight.

Is the whole house like this? I asked.

My family nodded.

Can we get out? I asked.

My family shook their heads.

Mom's eyes were watery. Dad's mouth was a short, worried dash. Aggie's fingers were knotted in her hair, as if she were trying to pull it out, like we'd pulled out the vines.

We went downstairs. The door to the kitchen was closed. But I could see more green tendrils creeping in from the space underneath. All our work: undone. If we could open the door, I know we'd find a mass of leaves and green and flowers and pumpkins. Those big white pumpkins. From inside the kitchen, I could hear tapping sounds. Just like the ones I'd been hearing in my dreams . . .

Or at least <u>I'd thought</u> they'd been dreams.

Dad had found a small hatchet. He slashed at the vines coming in from the kitchen. But more appeared. We've closed off the living room and the dining room too—anywhere that's connected to the kitchen. Every window is covered with that gross green mesh. Mom pulled at the front doorknob, but it wouldn't budge. The phone is dead. So is the electricity. It's getting hot in here. And there's a bad smell, like when you leave spinach in the refrigerator for too long and it turns to slime.

(Later) Aggie is standing at the front door in the entry hall shouting for help. Dad's been chopping at the wall in his bedroom, trying to cut through to the outside, to see if the vines are covering the whole house or just the windows and doors. So far, he's only reached layers of insulation.

(Later) Thankfully, the clock at the base of the stairs is one of those wind-up kinds, so we can still tell time. It's getting toward evening now. My stomach hurts, but I won't tell Mom. I know everyone else is hungry too.

Sunday, July 22 (I think?), 1979

Writing this doesn't seem important anymore.

Maybe I'm wrong. Maybe writing is the <u>most important thing</u>. ~~It might be the only way anyone learns what happens to us.~~

Aggie keeps calling out for help. I have my door shut. Mom and Dad are in their bedroom. I found a radio that runs on batteries, and I've been listening to the oldies station and the news and the weather. It's so weird to hear the world going on outside as if everything is just fine.

What about us? Why is no one paying attention?

My stomach is grumbling. And the water coming from the spigot in the upstairs bathroom has slowed to a trickle. Thankfully the toilet still flushes. I can only imagine what's clogging up the pipes.

I want to stay asleep. Will someone wake me when this is over?

(Later) Aggie's missing!

When I turned off the radio, I noticed that she'd stopped yelling. I peered over the landing and saw that the front door was swung wide, as if she'd managed to yank it open. A few green tendrils were spilled inside onto the floor, but the wall of leaves and spiky vines was still blocking the way out. Mom and Dad came running. We screamed for my sister, but she didn't answer. Did she make it out? Is she searching for help? I hope I hope I hope so because if that's not the case, I don't want to imagine another case. Mom is crying and Dad is oozing sweat (or is it weeping?) and I'm more scared now than ever.

We closed the door to keep those tendrils from coming any closer. Now I'm cowering on Mom and Dad's bed. I don't want to be alone any longer.

(Later) There was a loud cracking sound. We raced out to the hallway and saw that the front door had broken in half. The vines are reaching across the room already, almost to the bottom of the stairs. The yellow flowers are huge. They look like they're glowing. Their bases are like balloons about to pop. Dad's hacking away, but the vines are thicker now. Like tree roots.

(Later) I barfed. I aimed for the trash bin under my mom's bedroom mirror, though why my brain insists <u>that</u> matters at the moment I don't know. I'm not sure <u>anything</u> matters anymore.

The thing is, Dad's gone.

He'd said he had a plan. He'd told me and Mom to follow him down to the entry hall, so we did. We stepped over vines that squirmed like monstrous worms right before our eyes. Dad said we could get out through the basement. Mom got mad.

That's your plan? she asked.

I agreed. Why would the basement be different than any other part of the house?

Dad looked confused. Tired. He opened the basement door. Mom and me stepped back.

Vines spilled out. Tendrils twirled around his ankles. They yanked his feet out from under him.

The rest is a blur. Did I imagine it?

What I remember: the color GREEN twining his body. I remember the sound of screaming—mine or his, I'm not sure. Mom tried pulling the plants away. But then they came for her too. She stumbled back. The vines retreated down the cellar steps into the darkness, and they took Dad with them.

I don't want to think about what happened next.

I can't.

And I don't want to imagine Aggie—

Me and Mom ran up the stairs to her bedroom.

The vines made it halfway to the second floor.

I think I'm going to barf again. Do people barf in dreams?

Mom was crying for a little while, but she's stopped. I've asked her a few times what we should do, but she won't answer. She just keeps staring at the closed bedroom door.

There are noises in the hallway. I feel like I'm alone here, even though she's right next to me.

(Later) MOM OPENED THE DOOR. She planted her feet and the vines spilled in. I was sitting on the bed, holding my flashlight and notebook and pen. I screamed. They took her. They took her away!

I'm so angry I can barely write this. She opened that door, knowing what would happen. Knowing she would leave me behind. I hate her. I'm sorry for saying that, because I love her and I always will, but right now I hate her more than anything.

I grabbed what I could (a pillow, a blanket, my notebook, the flashlight) and ran for the closet. I slammed the door and shoved the pillow into the space beneath. To keep out the volunteers.

I don't know what to do I don't know what to do I don't know what to do

Date unknown, July (?), 1979

Time is weird in the dark. I don't have a clock. I don't have my radio. It feels like my whole world is this paper and this pen and this flashlight. And the light's already started to flicker. I'm so thirsty.

Will someone find me after I'm gone? Will they find this notebook?

I've been reading through it in reverse, looking for a clue of when and why this started. I <u>think</u> I've found the answer, way back at the beginning. I'm surprised but also not surprised. I mean, Nico did warn us about the Bowens. I'm truly sorry for what we did or didn't do to them or <u>for</u> them.

When I close my eyes, I picture my family from a few weeks ago. Mom at the grill. Dad mowing the lawn. Me and Aggie kicking the soccer ball around the backyard. I can smell the burgers and hear the ice clinking in the cola glasses and the peeping tree frogs as evening arrives. How did all of it change so fast? I go back further, to when me and Aggie used to play with her dolls. I always had the one named Laura, and Aggie had the one called Ephraim, and Dad said we should play with the opposite dolls because boys are boys and girls are girls, but we laughed at him like he was a dummy so he gave up. I think about sitting at the old high chair—the one that Aggie broke but then Mom fixed with wood glue—and eating those French-style canned green beans that I hated and then ended up loving. And about when Mom threw all the Tinkertoys all over the place because she was mad that we never picked up after ourselves. Then there were the times, like on holidays, where there was a fire in the fireplace and all the grandparents would come and it was chilly outside but we'd all go out for a walk in the woods anyway, our breath steaming like mugs of hot chocolate. How funny it was that

Gramma always insisted it was called <u>hot chocolate</u> and NOT <u>cocoa</u>.

Is Gramma worried? She hasn't heard from us in what must be days now. Weeks? She can't be more worried than I am. I hope she doesn't come. They might get her too.

There's been that tapping at the closet door, just like how I used to dream about. But they're here now, for real. The volunteers. I can hear them as I write this.

<u>Tap-tap-tap. Tap-tap-tap.</u>

I know what's next. I've already seen it. Aggie. Dad. Mom. I don't like being alone. I don't like being one flashlight flicker away from total darkness.

Seconds feel like minutes. Minutes like hours. Memories take me backward and forward like my brain is a time-machine roller coaster.

The only place I know I can't reach is the future.

I'm so thirsty. I want to open the door.

The <u>tapping</u> is louder now. Almost a banging. No. That's not the word. It's like something is coming. Something big.

Something with spikes.

Something horrible but also . . .

Somehow beautiful.

Something that will take my breath away.

NITE CRAWLERS

⟶⟶⟶⟶⟫⟪⟨⟨⟨⟨⟵

Vera Hathorne had started fishing at Ferry Lake with
her older brother, Ray, soon after she was big enough
to hold a pole all by herself.

The summer Vera turned twelve, she entered the county-
wide Labor Day competition, determined to catch the largest
fish. Winning was in Vera's blood. Her daddy's dusty fishing trophies were proof. Momma kept them in a box in the
crawl space in the basement, and every so often, Vera would
go down and sneak a peek. More than almost anything, she
wished for a trophy of her own.

Almost anything.

During June of that year, Ray took Vera out in their daddy's old aluminum dinghy every morning just after dawn.
They'd turn off the engine and just drift, casting their lines,
not speaking, sometimes picking up middling kivers or perch,
but hoping always for trout or maybe the elusive largemouth
bass. She didn't mind keeping quiet in the boat on the lake.

She found the silence peaceful. Besides, all Ray ever wanted to talk about was girls, and Vera couldn't stand the ones he had crushes on. They always looked right through her.

If you drive the country highway near Ferry Lake, you'll see signs for NITE CRAWLERS. Some are hand-drawn—black marker on paper, taped up inside store windows. Others are painted on pressed wood and nailed to weather-worn telephone poles. Everyone who lives nearby knows that *nite crawlers* are *worms*.

But for bigger prizes, you need bait that's bigger than mere worms. The best fishers use a reflective lure or, even better, silvery, live minnows—items you can only get at fancy fishing shops. Since Vera had spent her savings on her fishing pole in May, she could only afford the cheap old nite crawlers that the gas stations advertised with their janky signs on the highway.

Out on the water, Vera hated reaching inside the dirty Styrofoam cups the station attendants handed her from behind their counters, and she loathed having to wrestle the wild wrigglers onto her hook. Sometimes, they bled.

One morning at the end of June, while the mist was burning off the water, Vera and Ray noticed another boat gliding silently a few dozen yards away from their own. A man was casting quietly. He looked a little older than her daddy would have been—salt-and-pepper hair and beard, laugh lines around his eyes, a crease between his brows. The man wore a red plaid button-down and faded brown cargo pants tucked into tall green rubber boots. He paid them no mind. His boat was a dinghy like theirs, only his was beat up, dented near the bow, and pockmarked with rust along the sides. Layers of paint had peeled away in sections, leaving strange spotted designs that reminded Vera of the opaque eyes of dead fish that floated occasionally near the shoreline.

As Vera watched, the man's fishing bob dipped. Ripples circled outward on the water's surface—an expanding bull's-eye. He yanked his grip backward, then began to reel in the line. The pole bent like a sapling in a storm. The man grunted, and his voice carried on the water, sounding as if his boat were only a few feet away. He pulled and reeled. Pulled and reeled. There was a small struggle. A bit of splashing. Then, up came the largest bass Vera had ever seen. The man looked over at her and grinned. He embraced the fish around its middle— the creature writhing violently—and then worked the hook from its mouth. Grabbing the fish by its top lip, he held it up for them to see. The bass looked almost two feet in length. Its silver, black, and green markings glistened. Its spine arched. Its gills pulsed.

Deep down, Vera wished for it to jolt from the man's grip and fall back into the lake. "Maybe we'll have better luck if we move closer to him," she whispered to Ray.

"Or maybe, all that splashing scared the bigger fish away," he answered. "Let's stay put." They went back to their own bobs, and the morning settled again into stillness.

A few minutes later, however, there came sounds of a second struggle.

This time, the man had caught a long silver pike. He struggled to hold up the fish, its meaty belly bulging over his fingers, its head and tail extending far beyond his grip. Thirty inches? More? The man's chuckling echoed to every pocket of the pond.

Vera smiled and gave him a reluctant thumbs-up.

The third fish that the man in the beat-up dinghy caught that morning was a rainbow trout big enough to feed a small family.

This time, Vera couldn't hold back. She shouted to him, "What's your secret?"

Ray threw her a warning look.

"Come again?" the man answered. He turned his engine's rudder, and the boat glided toward them.

"How are you catching such big fish?" Vera said once he was closer. "We're only finding bluegills this morning."

She could see the man clearly now. His wrinkles looked deeper than they had at a distance, and his skin was grimier, as if he hadn't washed in days. His eyes were a striking pale blue, and when he looked at her, Vera felt a shock of discomfort. A large bundle at the stern of his boat was covered by a piece of beige canvas, marked with oily stains. A second later, a stench made Vera dizzy. Rot. Chemicals. Dead things pulled up from the bottom of the lake. What was under that tarp?

"It's all about the bait, darlin'." The man smiled, showing yellow teeth with brown spots between them. Vera nearly toppled into the water, but her brother steadied the boat and caught her arm.

"And what kind of bait would that be?" Ray asked the man.

"Nite crawlers." The man sniffed. Something banged inside his dinghy.

"But that's what *we're* using," said Vera.

"Not like mine, I bet," the man said, "Mine are . . . *special*." He bent down and pulled a plastic container up from below. "You get yours out on the highway?"

Vera nodded, trying to keep her throat closed so she wouldn't smell that smell coming from his direction.

"*Right*," said the man, drawing out the word as if teasing her. "I get these from Mrs. Bowen up at Old Zion." He tilted the container toward Vera and Ray. His bait looked twice as large as theirs, almost like small eels. The creatures pulsed red, as if overfilled with juice. The glimpse made Vera's skin crawl. "The bigger fish love 'em. You put one of these suckers on a hook, the bass'll practically jump into your boat."

Vera scowled. "Are you doing the Labor Day Fish-Off?"

"I'm not so much for contests," he said. "A catch is its own reward."

"Where does the woman live again?" Ray sounded as intrigued as Vera. "Or is that a secret?"

The man laughed. "It's no skin off *my* back. I'm sure Mrs. Bowen would be happy to have you." He gave them directions to her house. Before turning his boat around, he added, "She ain't cheap. Might be worth it though if you plan on winning that fish-off, darlin'."

"I do plan on it," said Vera with a nod.

The man waved goodbye, then steered toward the bigger pond beyond this one, the three fish thrashing at the bottom of his dinghy.

"**How** much money do you have?" Vera asked Ray on the ride home.

He looked at her side-eyed. "You want to go up there?"

"If Mrs. Bowen's nite crawlers do what that guy says they do, then yeah. Absolutely!"

"I only have about forty bucks. And I need to make it last."

Vera knew what that meant: Ray needed money for dates with his girls. He worked at the ice-cream stand by the golf course, and they didn't pay much per hour because they said the staff would make it up in tips, but it turned out that just wasn't true. Vera was too young to have an actual job, and she only got allowance for chores when her mother had made a big commission at the furniture store where she worked.

"I wish I could help," said Ray. "Maybe in a few more weeks."

But Vera didn't want to wait that long. If she was going to win, she needed to start practicing with bigger bait right away and build up her strength.

That night, after Mom and Ray had gone to bed, Vera snuck down to the kitchen, where her mother's purse was hanging on the back of a chair. She dug around inside until she found the thick denim wallet. Inside were dozens of bills. How much would Mrs. Bowen's nite crawlers cost? Surely, Momma wouldn't notice twenty dollars missing. Vera folded one bill into her fist, then shoved the wallet back into the purse.

Slipping under her covers, Vera felt a strange ache in her stomach that made her sleep fitfully for the rest of the night.

In the morning, Ray took Vera out on the lake again. She said nothing about the money she'd stolen. Like the day before, they caught a few small fish, and once, Ray had a close call with something bigger, but it snapped his line before escaping into the deep.

Back home, Vera found an old map of Ferry Lake at the bottom of a drawer in her momma's room—one of the drawers that had belonged to her father before he'd gone away. Had it been a year yet? Daddy had worked in the scrapyard and loved getting dirty as much as he'd loved fishing. The detectives had said he'd run off, but Vera would never believe that, even when Momma told her she agreed with them. Apparently, her parents hadn't been getting along for some time. Plus, he'd done it once before, right after Ray was born. Vera spread out the map on the floor of her bedroom, searching for the roads that the man in the dinghy had mentioned would lead to Mrs. Bowen's house. Dragging her finger across the lines on the worn paper, Vera encountered a street labeled Zion Road. She followed this line in both directions until she came to a cross street called Old Zion. It was up in the woods on the ridge that overlooked Ferry Lake.

She was about to fold up the map when something caught her eye. There was a faint pencil mark on the paper near Old Zion. A very small X. Vera wiped her finger across it, and the X smeared. Who had put it there? Her daddy? Her grandaddy before him? How old *was* this map?

Vera rode her bike into the hills. Her legs ached as she pushed against the pedals. A few times, she had to swing herself off and march up an incline, guiding the bike beside her. When she reached Zion, her lungs were burning, her heart throbbing, and her hair was practically glued to her sweat-slick neck. She loosened the straps of her empty backpack. Here on the ridge, tall pines reigned. From where she stood, she thought she saw the turnoff down the slope before Zion Road curved sharply and disappeared into the trees. She could see no houses. The only residents seemed to be the cicadas whose shrieks arrived in deafening waves. Vera checked her pants pocket, making sure the twenty-dollar bill hadn't slipped out. She took off down the other side of the slope. The warm air felt cool on her red cheeks. Soon, Mrs. Bowen's special nite crawlers would be hers. Afterward, she'd grab her fishing pole back home and ride to the public beach to see what she could catch. Hopefully, something monstrous!

Pushing over the rough gravel of Old Zion, Vera watched the day transform into sudden twilight. The pines were closer together, the branches heavy with needles. The air felt crisper, as if spring were lingering there.

Ahead, a driveway appeared. Beside it was a wooden mailbox perched on a pole made of old, knotted driftwood. Nailed to the pole was a sign. NITE CRAWLERS 4 SALE. For a moment, Vera worried that it had been a mistake stealing Momma's money. But then she remembered her daddy's trophies. How proud she'd been of him when he'd won. How proud he'd be of her if he discovered she'd achieved one of her own. She pressed the pedal so hard, she nearly spun out.

The path was thin and overgrown, with a stretch of brown grass running up its middle. Tire treads on either side looked like they hadn't been touched in some time. When the house appeared, Vera skidded to a stop, her jaw opening like a . . . well, like a fish. The building was larger than she'd expected. Much larger. It reminded Vera of the old mountain houses her family would drive by on their way home from Catskills vacations. Three stories tall. Clapboard siding faded so deeply it had turned almost black. A pitched gray roof made of lichen-crusted slate. A wide front porch wrapped around the side. What surprised Vera the most was that many of the windows were bandaged up with shutters. Only a few were left open so that whomever stood inside might catch a glimpse of someone approaching.

Someone like Vera.

There was no car in the driveway. Nothing indicated that anyone was home.

Vera moved up the front walk, pushing through overgrown grass that reached up to her knees. She leaned the bike against the front steps. She took them slowly, pausing slightly with every creak, peering at the few open windows along the porch for a sign of movement. A rusted iron knocker shaped like the head of a fox hung in the center of the door. She lifted the fox's snout, then let it drop. A resounding CLACK echoed into the yard. But still there was no sign of movement inside.

She tried again, knocking the fox head three times. The only response came from the shrieking cicadas. Vera looked down at her bike. She couldn't just leave. Could she?

Vera grasped the brass knob. The metal was so cold, she felt it in her teeth. She pushed, and a moment later, she was staring into shadow. She couldn't make out much—a thin foyer with gray floral wallpaper and a steep staircase climbing to the second floor.

"Hello?" she called out. Stepping through the entryway, Vera encountered a wall of freezing air. And the smell . . . It reminded Vera of the man from the boat yesterday morning. "Mrs. Bowen?" A dark runner led down the hallway beside the stairs. The rug cushioned Vera's steps. "My name is Vera Hathorne. I'd like to buy some nite crawlers." She waited, then added, "I'm sorry to barge in, but I—"

A clattering came from below. A tool falling from a shelf? A door banging against a wall? An oopsie-daisy with a cup of tea?

Well, that explains it, Vera told herself. *That's where the woman is.*

The basement.

Ahead, a doorway opened onto a stairwell. The smell was stronger here. Vera had to grab the door frame to steady herself. Only a bit of daylight reached the bottom of the steps below. Vera swung her hand against the inside wall, but when she flipped a light switch, nothing happened. "H-hello?" she tried again, a shaky whisper. Almost every part of her was saying *turn around.* But then one small part reminded her of the contest.

Of the trophy.

The house was still now. Whatever made that clattering sound was gone. It had probably been a critter, Vera figured. A mouse. A chipmunk. A squirrel.

If that horrid stench from the old man's boat yesterday had been the nite crawlers, then maybe the bait was down there in the dark.

Where would Mrs. Bowen have kept a flashlight? Vera turned to find a dusty kitchen. Pale daylight streamed through an open window. In the cupboard below the sink, she found what she was looking for. The flashlight was long and silver and ancient. When she turned the metal knob at the end, it made a dim glow. Back at the staircase, Vera grasped the wooden railing and followed it to the bottom, where the darkness thickened like pitch. The beam illuminated a dirt floor.

Vera's temples ached. Her lungs felt too small. She would get out as quickly as possible. She shifted the light around the room. One wall was lined with shelves, stacked with knick-knacks. Glass jars. Metal boxes with hinged lids. Stray tools. Trowels and spades.

Where was the bait? Vera shined the light into the far-thest corner of the room, where several tables stood. Wooden crates sat atop them. They made Vera think of coffins.

A soft shuffling sound whispered from that direction.

Of the five crates, four were filled with the blackest earth Vera had ever seen. Only one sat empty. Flecks of mica and minerals glinted up from the crates that were full. She sensed the bigger nite crawlers moving just under the dirt, which bulged and shivered in a few isolated places. A film of sweat gathered on Vera's forehead.

Foolishly, she hadn't thought to bring a container.

She snatched a metal box from a shelf. Its contents rattled. Flipping open the lid, Vera found string and screws and eye-bolts and nails. She upended all of it onto the floor, wincing at the clatter that echoed off the walls, and then grabbed one of the hand trowels. Crooking the flashlight inside her elbow, she made her way back to the tables. Vera placed the metal box on the edge of one crate. Peering inside, she listened for the shuffling sound that had whispered moments earlier.

The dirt in one section broke apart slightly. Something was moving just below. Vera brought the trowel down, poking through the surface, just missing a bit of pulsating red flesh. The startled worm pushed itself deeper. "Oh no, you don't." Vera grunted, then reached with her free hand into the dirt. The worm jolted as she grabbed it, then writhed violently. Vera yanked it up from the bed and nearly screamed. The worm was almost a foot long, nearly as thick as her wrist. She swung the thing toward the metal box, but its tail (or its head) caught on the edge and knocked the container to the floor.

The nite crawler wrapped around her forearm. She tried to shake it off. "Ew!" Vera cried out. "Get off me!" She dropped both the trowel and the flashlight as she pulled the worm away and threw it into the metal box. She kicked the lid shut, then crouched with a sigh. After a moment, she realized that her arm hurt. She held up the flashlight. At the base of her palm, there was a tiny dot of red.

Blood?

Had the worm . . . *bitten* her?

From atop the table, there came an unexpected noise. A low, gravelly groan.

It sounded almost . . . *human*.

Vera raised the light, then brought herself slowly to her feet. The divot in the dirt from which Vera had stolen the nite crawler was a few inches deep. Something was visible at the bottom. Pale flesh.

But the nite crawler had been bright red.

Vera used the tip of the flashlight to widen the hole. The more she uncovered, the more confused she felt. Whatever was buried here was big. Maybe as big as the crate itself.

"*Errrrrghhh . . .*"

Vera leaped back. She focused the light. Then she saw it. Inside the hole. A milky eye. It blinked at her! She shrieked.

"*Help . . . me . . . ,*" said a voice from the hole.

Everything snapped into focus. A person was buried in the dirt.

Unsteady, Vera frantically tossed the earth to the floor. The trowel struck several of the giant worms, gouging them—red liquid making sticky mud.

Soon, she uncovered the person's face. Their head was hairless—no eyebrows or eyelashes. Cracked lips were blackened, drawn back from rotting teeth. Red welts appeared all over the translucent skin, wounds where the worms had sucked blood, or maybe, thought Vera through a tornado of panic, where they had burrowed inside.

Pinning the flashlight beneath her arm, she uncovered what felt like fishing line. It crisscrossed the crate, screwed into eyebolts on either side. Vera grabbed at the bindings, but the line was tight and strong. She was about to slice at it with the trowel when the flashlight dimmed. A second later, it blinked out.

The person in the crate moaned.

"I can't see," Vera whispered. "I'll go get help."

"Nnnnnooooo . . . ," the person answered.

But she'd already turned toward the staircase. She raced across the room and grabbed the rail, taking the steps two by two. At the top, she stumbled out into the hall.

A silhouetted figure stood in the kitchen, clasping a rusted shovel to their chest. "I'm sorry," they said. Vera recognized the voice. The old man from the boat. "She promised to let me go only if I brought her more."

"More *what?*" Vera sounded like she was singing a soprano solo in the school choir. She glanced around for a way past him.

"Worm food," the man said, swinging the shovel.

When she came to, Vera found she couldn't move. Something was stinging her shoulders, her arms, her hips, and legs. The sides of her vision were blurry, but a dim light from somewhere nearby allowed her to see that she was lying inside a wooden box.

No, not a box.

A crate.

Overhead, cobwebs hung from the rafters. Vera struggled to sit, but that only made the stinging worse. In the faint light, she realized the pain was coming from being tied up in fishing line that pinched her skin. She felt at her sides for the trowel. It was gone.

Footsteps echoed, thick-soled shoes scraping along the dirt floor. Someone was down here with her. "Mister?" Vera said, her voice scraping her parched throat. "Please. My mother will be—"

A shadow appeared. It wasn't the man, but someone she'd never seen before. Greasy dark hair hung down, nearly long enough to brush against Vera's chest. Hollows marked the spots where eyes should be. The nose was merely two dark pits. And the mouth was a gray slice across what looked like wet clay. Skeletal fingers clung at the edge of the crate, sharp nails digging into the wood.

"M-Mrs. Bowen?"

The mouth opened, the stink of her breath like the smell of the worms. "Aren't you just the *sweetest*," her voice crackled.

"Let me go! M-my brother will be looking for me!"

"Oh, I hope so." It was difficult to tell in the dimness of the basement, but it looked like her mouth had curled into a smile.

Was the hairless man she'd uncovered still trapped in the other crate? Was he listening? Or had Mrs. Bowen already covered him up again?

"No, please," Vera implored, her skin prickling.

"My babies have been so hungry." The next part came out like the chorus of a nursery rhyme. "*No longer . . . No longer . . .*" Mrs. Bowen disappeared for a moment. There was a grating sound, and then she was back, holding a trowel. When she turned it upside down, dirt spilled onto Vera's chest.

"What are you doing? Stop!"

There was more scraping. More dirt. The weight of it made Vera want to scream, but she kept her lips pressed tight because more dirt came and then more. It filled the spaces along the walls of the crate. It got into her hair and into her nose. Vera coughed and choked and turned her head to the side. She held her breath. Held her voice. Held it all inside. She struggled against the fishing line, ignoring the sting. If she tried hard enough, surely she'd break through. She'd grab that shovel from Mrs. Bowen, and then—

"Veee-raaaah . . ." The whispering was like flint striking flint in her mind. Was it the voice of the person in that other crate? There was a spark. How did she know them?

The spark ignited. How did they know her? In her mind, the flame illuminated the pencil mark on the map she'd pulled from her daddy's drawer. She imagined all his fishing trophies, packed away, gathering dust. He'd been so good. A real winner. They'd said the need to win was in his blood. Didn't that mean it was in Vera's blood too?

Scrrrrrape. Thump.

"Daddy?" Vera shouted back.

No answer came.

Mrs. Bowen went away for a few seconds, and when she returned, she held a glass jar. Inside, plump red things wriggled and writhed. Mrs. Bowen held the jar to her mouth and sang, *"Hungry babies . . . Hungry babies . . ."*

She turned the jar over, and the nite crawlers dropped onto the fresh dirt inside the crate. Her eyes as wide as heavens, Vera watched them burrow into the soil and twitch as they brushed up against her body. Mrs. Bowen reached toward Vera, gathered two fistfuls of dirt, and pushed them into Vera's face. She was kind enough, however, to leave space around her nose.

Even with her ears packed, Vera could still hear the nite crawlers moving through the box. It sounded like they were whispering, telling one another where to find flesh and bone. Her heart pumped blood, faster and faster. *Ray is coming,* she told herself. *Ray will save me. I'll get out of here, and I'll catch the biggest fish in Ferry Lake and they'll give me that trophy and I'll pay back Momma and everything will be fine.*

Something poked her side. There was a pinch between her ribs. Vera flinched.

Another poke, another pinch.

On her hand.

By her knee.

Her ankle, her neck, her cheek.

Another and another and another.

"Veee-raaaah . . ."

Seconds later, the sucking began.

AMELIA AT NIGHT

"No, no, no, no, no," Amelia whispered after she'd read the final line aloud. *"That's* enough of *that."* She tried to blink away the image of the giant red worms, but they had already scrabbled into her mind. "So gross!" Win wouldn't sleep tonight. She'd have to beg him not to tell their mothers why.

But when she looked up, Amelia found the other leather chair uninhabited. She glanced around the room. Her brother was gone. *"Wiiiin?"* she called out, loud and long.

The library was quiet. Quieter than it had been. Darker too. An inkiness had seeped into the room. The lights in the long hallway were off, and outside, the sun had set. The trees that had been reaching toward the rear of the library in the afternoon were now devoured by shadow.

Where had the time gone? Her mothers must be worried. *"Wiiiiiiiin?"* Amelia tried again. Had he wandered to the children's room without her noticing? But he'd been so interested in the scary stories. And where was the librarian?

Mrs. Brown . . . Shouldn't she have come around and warned them that the library was about to close?

Was it about to close?

Amelia clutched the book and ran up the corridor to the lobby. No one was at the circulation desk. A skeleton crew of antique lamps kept the space lit, but barely. In fact, the library was empty.

"*Wiiiiiiiin?*" She tried turning the knob at the front door.

Locked.

The librarian had forgotten to make sure everyone had left before closing up. Amelia shoved the ends of her hair into her mouth and began to suck nervously. She told herself that mistakes could be fixed. *Find a phone. Call Mama. Someone will come and let me out.* Still, that wouldn't answer where Win had disappeared to. She'd known something was wrong with that book, and she'd put her brother in danger. And now he was gone. The tips of her hair were sopping with saliva. She squeezed them out, wetting her fingertips and wiping them on her pants. But was Winter *gone* like Grandmother, she wondered? Or just regular *gone*? Like, to the restroom? After everything she'd considered over the course of the afternoon (evening?), she had a bad feeling about the type of gone that he was.

Amelia stepped on something and nearly yelped. She picked up the object and held it to a light. It was a small, flat piece of plastic, attached to a metal clip with a shoelace-like cord. Mrs. Brown's face stared up from the identification lanyard. Only now, her name wasn't Mrs. Brown. The letters peering up at Amelia spelled out *Mrs. Bowen.* Just like she'd first thought when she'd entered the library. Bowen? Amelia looked closer, examining each letter. Had they somehow switched back? Or had the librarian lied? Had she somehow made Amelia see what wasn't there?

And if so, then was this *her* doing? Alone. Locked in the library. Her little brother missing.

Just like Grandmother?

An engine revved, sending Amelia's heart up her esophagus. Looking out the window, she noticed a long car idling at the curb. The driver's door slammed. She stumbled back against the checkout desk. Thick exhaust belched from the tail pipe, lit by the streetlight overhead. Was someone watching her? Nearly out of breath, she was suddenly glad that the library was locked.

She grabbed for the phone that sat on the circulation desk beside the computer's keyboard. She was about to punch in her mama's number when she realized that there was no dial tone. *Of course. Why would there be?* Amelia wanted to slam the receiver down but managed to take a deep breath instead, which helped control her rising panic. Placing the phone back in the cradle, she heard a soft ticking. A circular clock hung over the doorway that led back to the reading room. When Amelia noticed how late it was, she gasped.

Three in the morning? The clock has to be wrong. Right?

The engine revved again. Her panic came rushing back. Her skin prickled.

What was a car doing out on the street at *three a.m.*?

Amelia glanced at the book which she'd laid on the desk. Seeing the faded cover again made her brain feel slightly numb, as if the pages had been laced with poison and its toxins were finally kicking in, making her see things, feel things, that weren't real. Mrs. Bowen? NO, it had been *Mrs. Brown.* She was sure of it. Wasn't she? Besides, what kind of monster would *poison* a book?

Then again, in the Baby Witch tale, there'd been mention of a book whose stories could come to life. There'd been a car belching exhaust like the one outside that had stolen away a boy.

No, no. This can't be . . .

Amelia noticed the bundle of balloons tied to the back of the desk chair. She remembered those bells she'd heard all afternoon.

These are only stories. This is only a book . . .

In a corner of the lobby, a dim orange bulb lit a thin glass case that stood a little taller than herself. Four shelves inside held sculptures made of white clay.

Not real. Not real!

Amelia inched closer. Her throat began to close up. She tried to swallow but couldn't. A few of the forms stood out to her: a mushroom man, a turtle, a T. rex.

I'm dreaming, she thought. *I fell asleep in the leather chair and these stories got in my head and that's where they've come to life. In my imagination. It doesn't feel like a dream. But do dreams ever really feel like dreams?*

"Wake up," she stated harshly. Nothing changed. She was still in the library's lobby. In the night. Surrounded by artifacts from the book she'd been reading. Hadn't someone in one of the stories she'd read pinched themselves when they'd thought they'd been dreaming? Amelia tried that, squeezing the flesh on her hand between her thumb and forefinger.

OUCH!

Now her hand ached.

This isn't a dream.

A whistling broke the quiet. Like her little brother's breath forced through his front tooth gap. The sound had come through the doorway on the left. Warmth flushed Amelia's scalp. Relief. He wasn't *gone* after all. In fact, it sounded like he might even be messing with her. The cretin.

A sign overhead read FICTION.

"Winter?" she whispered through a clenched jaw. "Come out of there." He didn't answer. Maybe he was scared too. "We have to go," she added breezily, as if nothing was wrong, and it wasn't the middle of the night, and the scary stories she'd spent the day reading weren't actually coming true. "The phone at the front desk doesn't work. I need to look for another one." It was easier to feel anger than fear—more comforting too. With a huff, she went through the doorway. The new room was filled with bookcases. "I'm counting to three and then I'm leaving. Up to you." Another moment of silence. "Mom and Mama are going to hear all about this, buddy boy."

But that only made her worry about why her moms weren't looking for her. If she'd actually lost track of time, if it were actually after three in the morning, wouldn't there be a search party? Emergency trucks? She looked out to the street again. Maybe she hadn't seen the car out there properly. Maybe it *was* Mom and Mama after all.

But no . . . There it was: a long sedan. Totally unlike their SUV. It belched another cloud of smoke.

Amelia let out a slow breath, trying to keep her brain from twirling out of her skull and hitting the ceiling.

Why wasn't Win answering her?

Unless, he hadn't been the one who'd whistled . . .

Something moved behind one of the bookcases. Amelia tensed. "Winter?" Coming around the corner, she caught a glimpse of someone as they disappeared around the far side. "Winter!"

She peeked into the next aisle. Again, a shadow at the other end slipped out of sight.

But it had been much taller than Win. Could it be the librarian?

"Mrs. Brown . . . uh, *Bowen?*" Which name was it? Speaking them both aloud made Amelia's head hurt, as if she were admitting finally that the stories in the books were actually real.

A figure blocked the way back to the lobby. The dim light from the display case in the corner revealed a tall woman with stringy dark hair that clung to her skull. Amelia halted, certain her eyes were playing a trick. But the woman took a step toward her. She was barefoot, her feet blackened up to her ankles, her split toenails caked with grime. She held out her arms, as if presenting a gift. Two long earthworms squirmed vigorously in each hand.

Amelia shrieked and then backed into the aisle between the two closest bookcases. Something bumped her, and she turned to find a man. His black hair stuck up in chunks. The rubbery skin of his Halloween mask was gleaming white, his jaw slack, his eye sockets black holes. Something sharp glinted in his hand, just like it had in the clearing on the tarot card illustrations. Without thinking, Amelia pushed at his chest. The man stumbled.

Mindlessly, she raced around the corner. The worm-woman swiped at her, but Amelia ducked and ran the other way, bookcases strobing by, making her instantly dizzy. From the corner of her vision, she saw movement in each aisle, shadows careening toward her. She held back a scream. She was on autopilot. *Get out . . . Just go . . .*

Where the cases ended, a large table sat surrounded by four chairs. Beyond were a pair of French doors.

A way out . . .

She skirted the table, then grappled with unmoving door-knobs. A brick patio was just outside, and farther, the woods.

Break the glass!

When she turned for one of the chairs, she found the man in the mask and the worm-woman only steps away. "Get back!" she shrieked. "Leave me alone!" She pushed past them, then charged into the corridor.

Light spilled from the lobby's entry. Amelia was about to run that way when something emerged from the doorway. A greenish, glowing mist. Swamp gas? But no . . . Amelia watched with watery eyes as a form appeared inside of it. Stick limbs. Rib bones that stuck out like barbs. A canine skull with too many teeth and empty eye sockets. Its beauty threatened to freeze her solid with awe before fear made her move again.

Amelia dashed across the hall, through another doorway. This room was a mirror of the last. Another table stood before her, surrounded by similar wooden chairs. Beyond the set of French doors was a pathway to a parking lot. She grabbed the back of a chair. She was about to swing it at the glass, when she decided to try the knobs.

These doors swung open. Cold autumn air eddied around Amelia.

It shouldn't be this easy.

She stared into the night, arms enfolded around her ribs, her fingers clutching her jacket. A distant streetlight glowed.

Something large was moving between the trees across the lot, almost as tall as the trees themselves. An enormous head attached to a lengthy spine that stretched to the sharp point of a reptilian tail. Its skin was bone white. Turning to face her, its toothy grin chomped at her imagination, as she realized exactly what story this monster was from. White eyes flashed black.

It charged.

In that moment, she saw her brother's face in her mind's eye, covered in red that dripped from deep gouges. Bite marks. Acid churned in her stomach, and she nearly gagged. If Win was wounded, it was her fault. Amelia hadn't brought him back to Grandmother's when she should have. She'd continued reading the stories when she knew there was something strange about them. She'd been trying to do good, but what if that had only caused her to do bad? Or maybe . . . her throat closed up . . . maybe she hadn't been trying to do good at all? Maybe she'd wanted to hurt Winter . . . hurt her whole family . . . Maybe she'd wanted them to know what she really thought about clearing out the old house. She'd been angry, and maybe that anger had seeped out of her just like the stories had from *Tales to Keep You Up at Night* . . .

The ground shivered with each footfall. The creature's mouth gaped wide, revealing dozens of spiked teeth and a dark passage that went deep inside. Amelia threw herself backward, swung the doors shut, and ducked around a corner. The building shuddered. Glass crashed, spilling in a shockwave across the floor.

Amelia scurried into a farther corner and then curled into a ball. Her pulse pounded her eardrums.

After a few seconds of quiet, she lowered her arms and lifted her head, taking in this new hiding space. It was separated from the rest of the room by a long bookshelf. Only one fluorescent light glowed from the ceiling panel overhead. The carpet here was plush. Miniature chairs sat around tiny tables. Colorful posters adorned the walls. READING IS FUN and GET LOST IN A GOOD BOOK. Thin volumes stuffed the stunted bookcases. This was the children's section. "Win?" she whispered.

She forced herself to breathe slowly. She'd be no good to anyone if she couldn't think straight. She had to remember these details, so she could catalog them later like the photos she'd done for her yearbook pamphlet. So she could tell people what had happened here . . .

Amelia peered over the top of the bookcase divider. Where the French doors had been, there was now a ragged hole. Pieces of the wooden panes dangled from the frame, broken glass glinting. *Where had the monsters gone?* Amelia steadied herself, clutching the corner of the closest bookshelf.

Whap! Something fell to the floor. She'd accidentally knocked over one of the displays sitting atop the case—a picture book called *MAMA, THERE'S A MONSTER!* She fought stinging tears, wishing her mama and mom would come and save her. She was unprepared to deal with all this by herself. Wasn't she still a kid? Weren't there rules about these things? Shouldn't there be?

Amelia picked up the book to set it right, when she realized that she had no idea where *Tales to Keep You Up at Night* had gone. In the commotion, she'd lost it. *Good*, she thought. *I don't ever want to see that book again.*

Something behind the bookcase brushed at her fingers. Amelia jumped back. *MAMA, THERE'S A MONSTER!* toppled again. Then, one by one, each of the books in the case popped forward and fell to the floor. Something was moving against the wall. Amelia had to look closer, to find out what new horror she might need to fight. Green tendrils wriggled and writhed, spilling forward off the shelf, inching toward her ankles. *The volunteers . . .*

"Oh no," she whispered. "No, no, no."

All at once, books exploded from the cases. Thick vines gushed out and thumped around on the floor, as if hunting for her.

Amelia held her hands over her mouth. *Keep quiet!*

Tiny green spikes glistened. Furry leaves spread wide. Large orange flowers bloomed in seconds. Moments later, the petals drooped and shriveled, their bases bulging. Their increasing weight lowered the flowers to the carpet, where the budding fruit continued to swell.

Soon, Amelia was surrounded by enormous white pumpkins. They looked like bombs ready to go off. How many strides would it take to reach the passage where she'd entered this space? Four or five at least. *How quickly can these vines move?*

If she ran, would she be leaving her little brother behind? Again?

A tremor shook the room. Amelia leaped over one large vine that had curled up behind her heels, and then she reeled across the carpet. She bumped a pumpkin, and the closest vine reacted, rising up as if to catch her. She darted to the side, but her foot came down atop one of the leaves. She slipped and tumbled to the floor.

The vines were upon her—the acid-green tendrils spinning through strands of her hair, the meatier lengths curling around her calves and biceps. Squealing, Amelia yanked the tendrils from her scalp, pulling out some of her own locks. She sat up and unraveled one vine from her ankle as more tried to wrestle her back to the ground. "Leave! Me! Alone!"

The floor shook again, this time with a frightening force, as if someone were pounding with a sledgehammer from below. The vines stopped moving. They relaxed their grip on her, then retreated back to the bookshelves from which they'd poured.

Relief coated Amelia in a cool chill before terror seized her again.

BOOM!

Something else was coming. Something big.

BOOM!

She scrambled to her feet.

BOOM!

The floor by the wall heaved upward. A crevice reached into the center of the room. Then, the carpet dipped down, floorboards snapping. Amelia wobbled, struggling to keep her balance.

BOOM!

The carpet slipped again, bringing Amelia to her knees. A moment later, something yanked the carpet down into the widening gap. Amelia was flung onto her back. A few white pumpkins tumbled into the void. Disappeared. Then there came a roar like nothing Amelia had known. She scrambled away from the hole.

SMASH!

Wood splintered upward. Cracks spidered across the walls. Chunks of ceiling plaster rained down. Through the dust, Amelia saw something emerge through the floor—some kind of monstrous arm. Its skin was striped black and white with multicolored pompom-like bumps, and at its tip was a white-gloved mess of claws. Calliope music played, like at a circus, but Amelia couldn't tell if it was only in her head. The arm swung, opening the floor wider. Bookcases disappeared down into oblivion. Amelia wondered briefly if Grandmother had seen all of these things too? If this was what getting to the end of the book meant for the reader? Would Grandmother have known what to do to survive? Did Amelia? She crawled toward the exit from the children's section, but then the monstrous arm slammed onto the bookcase that divided the room. Books blasted outward. As loose pages fluttered in the air, Amelia noticed a new way out, straight through the broken bookcase.

Too frightened to dash into the night (and possibly the jaws of a T. rex), she stood and ran, past the table and chairs, back into the center hallway before skidding to a halt.

Dark figures blocked the exits. She imagined all the characters and monsters and ghosts from the stories she'd spent the day reading, terrified of which ones might be barring her path. She looked frantically for another escape route. A staircase dipped down to the basement, but dozens of balloons were streaming up from the darkness. The rest of the Happy Birthday Man must be down there—the part with all the mouths.

Bright laughter sounded from behind her. Turning, she discovered another staircase leading to the second floor. A whistling shriek came from above. *Winter!* He'd been hiding up there the whole time. He was calling out to her. He needed her to save him. Amelia took the steps two by two, thinking of that morning when she'd ventured to Grandmother's attic to escape from him. She didn't have to be the villain of the story anymore. If she reached him, if she managed to get them both out of this trap, she'd be the hero.

As Amelia reached the top step, she heard scrabbling sounds behind her. The hallway was almost entirely dark, with the only light coming through the edges of a closed door several feet away. She grasped the knob and pushed. A warm glow washed over her. She managed a strange pirouette and slammed the door shut. With a gasp and a whimper, she pressed her back against it, preparing for the beasts to counter with a crash and a shove and a—

But nothing came.

Amelia listened. The hallway was quiet.

It was then she realized she was not alone.

AMELIA IN THE ATTIC

Win's striped shirt and pants and shoes formed a dizzying patch right in the middle of Amelia's vision. His back was toward her, and his shaved head reminded her of a fuzzy peach. A tiny crystal lamp hung from the ceiling, casting streaks and rainbows onto the dingy beige wallpaper. A faded yellow curtain covered the single window in the far wall. He stood before a large brass bed. Patchwork covers rustled as a person hidden behind him shifted their weight. Another sound came—a ferocious gulping. Then, a weathered hand reached out and placed an empty glass on a side table, next to a small silver bell with a dark wood handle.

"*Winter*," Amelia stated forcefully. When her brother turned, he wore an amused look—his cheeks ruddy, his lips wet, his eyes wide with surprise.

"Hi, Amelia!" he said.

From behind him, propped on a pile of pillows, an elderly woman stared at Amelia. The woman sat up, her thick glasses slipping down her nose. She was dressed in a black nightgown, ratted ruffles at her neckline that looked like dead flower petals. Her mouth was a smile that was also *not* a smile.

"You found us!" Win chirped, as if they'd been playing a game all along.

"We have to go home," Amelia answered, struggling to move her mouth around the words.

"Oh, no, dear," the old woman answered. "Everything you were running from is right on the other side of that door."

"Who . . . who are you?" Amelia asked.

Win laughed in surprise. "You don't recognize her? This is my granny!"

"*Your* granny?" Amelia shuddered, feeling not quite right. "I—I've never seen her before."

"You don't have to have *seen* someone to *recognize* them," Win answered. "You've read her story. She exists now." He touched his forehead. "In here."

Amelia's lungs burned from the chase. Her mind was a tornado of images; some of them reached out to her, swiping with claws as they spun by. She pressed her feet into the floor, trying to solidify her stance in this weird new world. "What are you *talking* about?"

"This is my *granny*," Win repeated slowly, as if speaking to a very young child. Amelia shook her head, confused. "Ah, you don't recognize *me* either." Win smiled. "Everyone knows that there are witches out in the woods," he whispered. "They tend to look like you and me. More like *me*, at the moment."

"I—I don't understand." Amelia's voice cracked. She moved to the corner of the room. She wanted to be as far away from her brother and this strange woman as possible.

"You wouldn't, now, would you? This disguise has been pretty good. One of my best . . . right, Granny?"

"Yes, child." The voice was warm and full of life.

"Who are you?" she asked her brother.

"Let me make it easier for you," he said. Amelia blinked, and suddenly Win wasn't Win anymore.

This was a girl who appeared to be about Amelia's age. She wore strange clothes: a raggedy brown dress, shiny silver stockings that went up over her knees, a cluster of brightly colored ribbons tied at her wrists, black boots that were caked with dried mud. Her dark hair was long and curly, fairly greasy, and it was tied up on the top of her head with another ribbon—this one acid green. Amelia noticed blue markings on her neck. Drawings maybe?

Beware, beware . . .

Amelia felt herself go numb. "You're . . . the Baby Witch."

The girl laughed. Wide-mouthed and clumsy and swooping and silly. "What a funny thing to call someone." Her voice was low; *velvety* was the right word for it. "I mean, *clearly* I'm no baby. Not anymore, anyway."

"But that's who you are," Amelia answered. In the story, Bethany had shrunk back from the girl, but Amelia wasn't going to play games. *"The Baby Witch.* From the story." Her voice had fight in it. It felt good to know the girl could hear it too. Amelia stepped forward. "Where is my brother?"

"Oh, calm down. He's been at your grandmother's house with your mommies all day."

"But—"

"It was me the whole time." The girl smiled, holding back laughter. "Whistling in the children's section. Curled up on the seat across from you. Begging for the rest of the stories. Forcing you to read them all."

"Then *this*—" Amelia glanced at the door where the monsters had chased her. "It's *your* fault?"

"I played my part," answered the girl. "Just like I always do." She held up the book—the cloth cover a faded red, almost pink. Embossed in silver on its side was a long title that appeared blurry in the dim light. *Tales to Keep You Up at Night.* "I would put most of the blame on my siblings. They're the ones who made this."

"Your siblings wrote the book?"

"They didn't write it, silly. They *made* it."

Granny chuckled and then coughed. "Very special. Just like you, dear." She held out her hand. The girl reached for the water glass on the side table, which was suddenly full again, and gave it to the old woman.

Amelia didn't understand. "Where is my grandmother?"

The girl cocked her head playfully. "And here I am thinking you're smarter than this. You've read the stories. Do you really need me to connect *all* the dots for you? Where's the fun in that?"

Amelia clenched her fists. "What did you do to her?"

"You already know the answer."

Amelia squeezed her eyes shut. But then the dinosaur's maw appeared, the vines pouring from the bookshelves, the hole in the floor where the calliope music was playing. She opened them again, shaking the images away. "H-how could you?"

Calmly, the girl helped her granny finish her water and then held the old woman's hand. "Let me ask you something . . . What would you do for your family?"

"My *family*?" Amelia imagined her mom and mama. And Winter. And Grandmother. A sudden worry stabbed at her ribs. "What have you done to them?"

"Answer my question."

Amelia wanted to fly at the girl, to throw her to the ground, to pound at her. She'd never hit anyone, ever, and she'd never planned to. But right now . . . *Right now* . . . She couldn't control the emotions buzzing through her body. "Anything," she said, tears in her eyes. "I'd do anything for them."

The girl gave a small grunt. "Funny. So would I." She held up the book again. "This is my *anything*—my way of keeping my family alive." The girl sat on the bed next to her granny. "I know you know what I mean. Your own grandmother has been gone for more than a year. When her house is sold, a part of her will disappear forever. The experiences you had there, the stories . . . You think your memory will hold them. But it won't. Piece by piece, she will fade into shadow. Judge Turner threw away so much of my history when he tossed that book into Moll's Well. When it comes to memory, my family isn't so different from yours." The girl glanced down at the book. *The tales* . . . "What is a memory if not an idea. A feeling. An emotion. A sensation. If people read this book, the idea of my family echoes, our love and hate and fear and hope resounding in other people. If only for a night, we can live again. All of us." Granny leaned forward and whispered something in the girl's ear. The girl smiled. "That's right . . . And if the ideas *don't* spread, then at least we can eat."

Amelia pressed her arms against the walls, steadying herself in the corner. "You're going to *eat* me?"

The girl glanced at the old woman, who let out a soft chuckle. "We might." The girl looked to the door. "We could also share you with the others." She considered. "Not a whole lot of meat on those bones, but it doesn't take much to fill us up. Never has."

Amelia thought of Grandmother. Of Grandfather. Of what had happened to them. *We can eat.* She whimpered. "Please . . ."

"There's another option." The girl cocked her head, her hair flopping to the side. "We let you go." Amelia felt faint. "You'll appreciate that, won't you? You'll appreciate me if I saved you from the rest of my family."

"Yes, yes, of course, yes."

"And you'll tell *your* family about us. About the Bowens and the Turners and the others who stole our legacy. And especially about what happened *here*?"

Amelia swallowed. "They'll think I've lost my mind."

"But you'll tell them? You'll appreciate my kindness?"

"Yes." Amelia would have said anything to get away. "Of course I will."

"Good," said the girl. "Because ideas only spread when we share them." She sounded suddenly cheerful. It was strange how she looked so young but must have been very, very old. Even if she'd been the youngest of them, this girl was no *baby*. "One last thing," she said, sliding off the bed. "You'll take this book." She held it out. "You'll put it somewhere you know someone will find it."

"But . . . won't reading the stories bring them to life again? Will what happened to me tonight happen to them too?" And suddenly, it made sense. *Grandmother . . .*

"That's the whole point, silly! The Bowens will live on. And on. And on."

A coldness came over Amelia. How could she dare put someone else through this? It was clicking into place. *That* was what had happened to Grandmother. And Grandfather before her. Amelia had her answer. They had done the selfless thing and decided to keep the book hidden, refused to pass it on to another unsuspecting victim. *You've read the stories*, the girl had said. *Do you really need me to connect all the dots for you . . .*

What price had Amelia's grandparents paid to keep the rest of the family safe?

You already know the answer.

"You'll do this for us," said the girl. "Because if you don't, we can come back. And you go away . . . forever. If there is one deed that witches love, it's revenge. Take the book and go."

DO NOT READ THIS BOOK.

Amelia felt her arm extend toward the girl, toward the book, as if her fingers had been magnetized. They closed around the cover, the faded fabric feeling like an old and beloved blanket, something you might return to again and again for an echo of an almost forgotten feeling.

As soon as the girl let go, the room went dark.

Amelia glanced around, her eyes adjusting to the murk. There was no brass bed, no chandelier glistening from the ceiling, no Granny, no glass of water, no bell. Wooden roof beams reached up from the edges of the floor, congregating at a seam high over her head. A brick chimney rose through the center of the room, the dust of its crumbling mortar lying in a scattered halo. Amelia's shadow stretched across the wooden planks of the floor. Behind her, a small lightbulb hung over the top of a steep set of stairs. The smell of the place brought her back into her body, and suddenly, she knew where she was.

Grandmother's attic.

She was standing in the exact spot as when she'd picked up the book that morning. There was a whooshing sound as the memories of the day, of the stories, swirled through her head. Or maybe it was the wind against the roof. *How did I get home?* But she knew.

She knew . . .

She was that doomed pilot, her namesake, rescued from a fateful flight, brought back to the wider world, given a second chance. She was Alice, the Pevensie children, Coraline, Dorothy—characters from books her mothers had read to her when she was younger, from stories that were more frightening than anyone liked to give them credit.

Amelia glanced at the book in her hand. How had it gotten up to the attic in the first place? Had the librarian—one of the Bowens—snuck into Grandmother's house and left it for the Turner-Ingersolls to find? One more family of Judge Turner descendants to torture? Or had Grandmother tried to hide it? But then, what about her dream? Grandmother had practically pointed the way back to the book. Unless the person in her dream *hadn't* been Grandmother. Amelia knew now that the Bowens could use faces that did not belong to them. Could they also use handwriting? *DO NOT READ THIS BOOK.* She burned with foolish shame. She cursed herself, and then whoever wrote the note; everyone knows there's no better way to get someone to do something than warning them against it. She wanted to toss the book into the shadows. She almost did, but then she remembered what the girl had said: *We can come back.*

Trembling, Amelia made her way down the steps as fast as she could manage, into the daylight of the second floor's hallway.

AMELIA AFTERWARD

Downstairs, things were as they'd been before—Mom in the foyer with the cardboard boxes, Mama with the dishware in the kitchen. Somewhere in a distant part of the house, Win was whistling. When Amelia heard it, waves of relief almost knocked her off her feet.

"What have you got there?"

Trembling, Amelia held the book to her side. "Some old book I found in the attic."

"You gonna read it?"

"*No*," Amelia practically shouted before calming herself. "I mean, I already have *so many* books. Not enough time for this one."

"Wanna stick it in one of the donation boxes?" Mom asked.

Amelia thought of what the strange girl had said. *You'll tell your family about us. About what happened here . . .* "I think . . . I'll hold on to it for now."

"Suit yourself." Mom turned to the box she'd been packing.

Tell your family . . .

Amelia opened her mouth to speak, but nothing came out. She thought of what would happen if she shared the story of what she'd been through. The night at the library. The book that brought monsters to life. The girl who'd pretended to be her little brother. Learning what may have *really* happened to Grandmother. And to Grandfather before her . . . What they'd both done to protect the rest of them. How they had not given in to the Bowens' threats. It was almost too much to bear.

Mom sensed her hesitation. "What is it, sweetheart?"

"Nothing," she whispered, knowing deep down that it was the wrong answer. The girl's voice echoed in her memory: *You'll appreciate me?* "I miss Grandmother. It's hard watching her things disappear."

Watching *her* disappear, was what she'd really meant, especially now that she knew why it had happened.

Mom extended her arms. "Come here." Enclosed in a hug, Amelia couldn't hold back any longer. Tears soaked her mom's T-shirt. She shook with sobs.

Footfalls approached from the kitchen. "Excuse me," said Mama. "Why was I not invited?" She knelt beside them and joined in.

"Hey!" Win shouted from the top of the steps. "What about me?"

Amelia glanced up. Through blurred vision, she saw his stripes and peach-fuzz haircut. He was alive. Undamaged.

Unafraid. The same silly kid who knew exactly how to drive her up a wall, and she loved him for it. "Get down here, goofball."

"Goofball!" Win echoed. He laughed all the way down the stairs.

By the time everyone climbed into the SUV to head home, Amelia's body ached with exhaustion. She fell asleep, waking only when Mama pulled into their driveway, feeling grateful that she hadn't dreamed along the way.

Dinner came and went (grilled cheese sandwiches and bowls of tomato soup), and Amelia spoke not a word about the book that she'd already hidden, nor about the girl she'd promised to *appreciate*. They were home now. That was what mattered.

She kept her bedside lamp on throughout the night.

In the morning, she remembered what was lying underneath her bed. The book could not stay there forever. If she tossed it into the bin in the kitchen, Mom or Mama or Win might pluck it out. Anyone who read it would have to go through what Amelia had gone through. What Grandmother and Grandfather had gone through. No, she'd take it to school and then bury it at the bottom of the dumpster behind the cafeteria, where no one would ever read it. It was the right thing to do. Wasn't it?

Amelia walked alone along her usual route. Groups of kids passed by. Any other day, she would have tried to be social so that when she worked on the official yearbook next year, they'd know her name. Her face. They'd know to open up. To trust her. That was how you plant those kinds of seeds.

The sky was clear. The sun was warm. The air was crisp. Leaves rustled on the trees. Her backpack hung heavy from her shoulders, all of her assignments completed on time, as always.

Every assignment, Amelia thought, except for one.

She stood aside, leaning against the stone wall that bordered the cemetery. The further she moved from the moment when she'd discovered the book in her grandmother's attic, the more it felt as though she'd imagined the whole thing. If that was the case, the horrors *couldn't* hurt anyone. Opening her backpack, she plucked out the book. Had she even *read* it? The stories were inside her head (how could she forget them?), but if she'd never left the attic in the first place, if she hadn't sat in the library and turned the pages, then maybe none of it had *actually* happened. Maybe she'd *never* made that promise to the Baby Witch at all. *You'll take this book. You'll put it somewhere you know someone will find it.*

So then, what was the harm in keeping the promise after all? Just to be safe?

Her hand trembled as she opened the cover again. She flipped to the table of contents. All the titles were there. She remembered their stories as if she'd lived them herself.

But now there was another title at the bottom. A story she hadn't read. It was called "Long Overdue." How had she missed it? She found the page where this new story started. Taking a deep breath, she dared to read the first few sentences:

Amelia discovered the old book lying in a dark corner of her grandmother's otherwise empty attic. Its paper jacket was missing—the cloth cover a faded red, almost pink. Embossed in silver on its side was a long title that appeared blurry in the dim light.

Amelia threw the book with all her strength. It landed between the yellow lines out in the center of the street.

I'm still dreaming.

But Amelia knew she wasn't dreaming. *She* was in the book now—her own story was one that would keep someone up at night.

Or worse . . .

This was a warning.

We can come back. If there is one deed that witches love, it's revenge.

The seeds had sprouted. Soon they'd grow, like vines.

Amelia checked both ways, dashed out into the street to retrieve the book, then placed it by the crosswalk. Hiding around the corner at the end of the cemetery wall, she watched as another pair of kids came up the sidewalk. A brother and a sister. Several years younger than herself. They stopped as they noticed the object at their feet. The faded red cover. The white sticker on the spine containing catalog numbers from a library that did not exist. They didn't see Amelia watching.

"Someone must have dropped it," said the sister, glancing up and down the street.

The brother picked up the book. "*Tales to Keep You Up at Night?*"

"Ooh, I *love* scary stories," the sister exclaimed.

"We'll read them together," said the brother.

The two passed the edge of the wall where Amelia was hiding.

Those two aren't much older than Win, she thought. "Wait!" she called out, running after them. "Put it down! Leave it alone!" She raced up the sidewalk, her hair whipping her face, the ends catching in her mouth. "Stop!" she cried.

When she reached the corner, the brother and sister were nowhere to be seen.

Neither was the book.

The rest of the day passed as usual. Amelia turned in her assignments and her teachers gave her more in return. She ate lunch with Scotty and Georgia and never once brought up what had happened over the weekend. She sat through the last of her classes, trying to pay attention, but her mind kept coming back to the brother and sister from that morning. What if, when they read the tales, they weren't as strong as she was? Would they simply put the book down and leave it alone? Or would they read to the end? Learn its secret? Would they have to face the girl too? Agree to her terms? Keep the memory of the Bowens alive? Was that the only way to survive? Grandmother and Grandfather had thought not. And now they were gone.

Yet the book continued to exist.

The walk home felt lonelier than on the way there. More kids were out and about, running and laughing and playing, but none of them glanced at Amelia. What would they think if she called them over and told them what she'd learned? That ideas—good and bad—can take root and spread. That you have to be careful with the stories you tell. That monsters, *real monsters*, exist. That evil is real too, but sometimes—no, *often*, it does not look how you'd imagine it.

She found Win sitting alone on the couch in the den. His bus got him home quicker from his school than Amelia could walk from hers. "Heya, kid," she said, passing through on her way to the kitchen for a glass of iced tea. Normally, she might have mussed his hair and continued silently on her way. But things felt different now. "Do anything fun today?" When he didn't answer, she stopped. He was hunched over, focused on something on his lap. "Hello?" she tried again. "Winter?" Coming around the couch, she saw that Win was engrossed in a book. A corner of its cover was visible at the edge of the yellowed pages.

A faded red. Almost pink.

She rushed over and yanked it away.

"Hey!" he cried out.

She looked at the spine. Silver lettering glared at her. Amelia shrieked and flung the book across the room. It hit the wall beside the fireplace and landed in a potted fern.

There was a flurry of footsteps. The moms appeared in the doorway.

"What happened?"

"What's wrong?"

Win sat up on his knees. "I was reading and Amelia grabbed my book and threw it!" His lip quivered, as if she'd tossed *him* against the wall as well.

Amelia ignored her parents. She held Winter by the shoulders. "Where did you get that?" she demanded, giving him a shake.

"Amelia!" Mama answered, breaking them apart. "Stop it!"

But Amelia wouldn't stop. Dread was hollowing out her body so that it almost hurt. "Win! Answer me! Where did you get that book?"

Win held his knees to his chest. He was terrified of her. "Some kids gave it to me at school. They said that I'd *app*— that I'd *approp*—"

"*Appreciate* it," she finished for him. The words fell from her mouth like a half-chewed piece of meat.

"They gave it to me," Win answered. "It's mine!"

"Amelia, would you tell us what is going on?"

Amelia looked to the book, propped up in the pot, hidden slightly by the leaves of the houseplant.

If she'd done what the girl had asked, why had the book come back?

What would you do for your family?

Amelia remembered the promises she'd made. She'd kept one. But the other, she'd broken.

You'll tell your family about us. About what happened here? You'll appreciate my kindness?

Mama was gripping her shoulders now. "Why did you do that?"

Amelia tore herself away and stumbled to the fern. Reluctantly, she plucked the book from the soil. She held it up for all of them to see.

She'd wanted it to have been a dream. She'd wished for the horror contained within the pages to be fiction and fiction *only*. Some memories are faulty by design. But you can't force a memory, a tale, an idea to be untrue simply by wishing it so. Nor could you break a promise you'd made to a witch.

If there is one deed that witches love, it's revenge.

Amelia tried to imagine the strength her grandparents must have had to withhold the book from the rest of the family. But was strength enough to end an evil, a curse that circled and cycled and coiled through history like a snake eating its own . . . *tale?*

Winter was staring at her. Leaning toward her, as if waiting for the answer.

"Amelia?" Mama asked softly. "Is everything all right?"

Amelia looked into the faces of her family. Her grandparents came into her mind. Despite what she'd been through, despite what she'd learned, she wasn't sure she could be strong like them. But then . . . people were strong in different ways.

Her mom held out a hand, as if begging for her to speak. Amelia only clutched the book more tightly. She thought of everything she'd learned from reading the tales.

Maybe it wasn't strength she'd need to end the curse.

Maybe it was . . . knowledge?

Secret.

Ancient.

True.

A knowledge that twines through all the stories that connect us, like a worm or a snake or a tendril of smoke that squirms out of sight if you shine a light at it.

Old Moll's talents had come from studying her own past, from her family's legacy—that book of shadows. Since the time of her leaving, when Judge Turner had tried to take her land and her life, she'd discovered a way to let her loved ones live on. Maybe Amelia could do the same—right that wrong—if she held close to her curiosity and sought answers, knowledge, hidden in the shadows. Like Moll had done . . . and the rest of the Bowens.

"Amelia?" Mama asked again, quieter this time, worry radiating from her. "Sweetheart?"

Amelia considered another line from one of the tales: *Maybe, just maybe—you are the witch.* She wasn't entirely sure if she believed that, but she clung fast to the idea, that amid this cycle of destruction, she could find her own power, her own knowledge of the curse and how to break it. Maybe someday.

For now, there was another matter that needed attention.

Feeling weak, Amelia slumped to the ground, the book as heavy as lead. But then she straightened her spine and settled her legs against the floor, trying to find comfort in this strange new position. She glanced again to her family, who were staring back at her in wonder, as if little markings had appeared across her skin—squiggles and swirls and sigils, drawn in blue ballpoint ink.

Maybe, just maybe—you are the witch.

She took a deep breath and began. "I have a story to tell."